SIX-SHOOTER JUNCTION

Deputy Sheriff Sam Regan considered he had been lucky when he found an outlaw's horseshoe mark outside the Bankers' Hotel in Blackwood after a bank raid. He overtook a raider and was badly shaken to learn that the outlaw was Pete Arnott, a boyhood friend. The meeting, however, led to gun play and Sam had to kill Pete. He tried to hide the fact that Pete was an outlaw, but the truth leaked out to certain important people who insisted on Sam chasing the raiders and proving the link between Pete and the gang . . .

DAVID BINGLEY

SIX-SHOOTER JUNCTION

Complete and Unabridged

LINFORD
Leicester

First published in Great Britain in 1970

First Linford Edition
published 2005

British Library CIP Data

Bingley, David
    Six-shooter junction.—Large print ed.—
Linford western library
1. Western stories
2. Large type books
I. Title
823.9'14 [F]

ISBN 1–84395–839–2

Published by
F. A. Thorpe (Publishing)
Anstey, Leicestershire

Set by Words & Graphics Ltd.
Anstey, Leicestershire
Printed and bound in Great Britain by
T. J. International Ltd., Padstow, Cornwall

This book is printed on acid-free paper

1

The brassy sun was high in the sky. It was a little after eleven o'clock in the morning when Chief Deputy Sheriff Sam Regan began to approach the county town of Blackwood, in Basin County, west central Texas. The steaming hide of his sweating dun quarter horse bore testimony to the rate of travel the pair had sustained since leaving the lesser town of North Creek, shortly after breakfast.

In spite of the heat, Sam was keen to be back in the county seat. His senior, Sheriff Moses Wallis, a veteran lawman with a grey goatee beard, had been running a fever for the past couple of days, and the town marshal his opposite number, was out of town visiting kin on the other side of the Little Pecos river.

Knowing he was the senior fit peace officer in the county seat gave Sam a feeling of responsibility which he did not take lightly.

At twenty-six years of age, he was a tall, muscular young man with a lot of fair wavy hair and rather penetrating green eyes. His rather pointed face, and straight sharp nose, were liberally sprinkled with freckles, and the tiny blotches showed up well because he was habitually clean shaven.

In an effort to offset the drabness which perpetual trail dust imposed upon all, Sam was sporting a green shirt and a white bandanna. A shiny brown leather vest gave him a further touch of colour.

He was yawning and covering his open mouth with the back of his hand when a distant flurry of explosions, which could only be interpreted as gunshots, made him blink and shift his body in the saddle. The sounds had come directly from town. But what made them? Was there some gun happy trail herder letting his hair down at the town's expense, or were the shots fired in anger?

This was an ordinary working day of the week. There was no special reason he could think of for rejoicing. What was it, then? His mount was tired and he did not want to push it unnecessarily. So he willed himself to keep calm, and simply jogged towards the nearest of the buildings on the north side of town.

Three minutes later, a lithe young man, riding a shaggy pony without a saddle, came hurrying to meet him. This was a young orphan, known to all as Philip, who had somehow adopted the town and grown up in it.

'Hey, Sam, can you go a little faster? There's a rumour raiders have hit the bank, and the way things are you're goin' to be needed!'

'How do you mean about the way things are? And which bank are you talkin' about?'

Sam was at once curious and slightly aggressive. No sooner had he arrived within the town's environs than he was wanted all over again. Anyone would think that he ran both the sheriff's office and that of the town marshal.

Young Philip bit his lip. 'You know how it is, Sam. The Sheriff down with fever, an' the marshal still out of town. If you don't make some sort of move, nobody else will. It's the Banker's Hotel where the shootin' started, an' by what I've heard the bank in there does three quarters of the town's business in bankin'.'

Sam thought Philip had good ears and that he was probably right. The Holborn Hotel in the county seat was rather unique, in as much as it was the only hotel in the Holborn chain which had a bank located within its walls.

Brushing conjecture aside, Sam asked questions, seeking confirmation that a hostile strike had, indeed, been made against the bank in the Holborn Hotel. Philip was emphatic in his assertions that raiders had attacked the bank, and he was so far carried away with himself that he tried to turn his horse about

4

and arrive back in the danger zone ahead of the deputy.

With his mouth set in a grim line, Sam used his rowels. The tired dun found a new lease of life, and gradually drew away from the saddleless pony. Soon the hard-worked animal was carrying its master across the vacant lots and through the alleys of the north side of town, making a bee-line for the sheriff's office on Main.

Second Street was reasonably calm, but when the dun emerged on Main, some two or three score of people of all descriptions were milling about in the 'safe' area near to the sheriff's office. All eyes turned in Sam's direction. Some men started to shout advice, others were content to acknowledge that he had arrived, and that he looked to be in a businesslike frame of mind.

'Down at the intersection, about five minutes ago, Sam,' one breathless old man called. 'We caught a glimpse of them as they came away. If you ask me, they rode off towards the south! It always helps to know what direction they head in!'

Another man was saying, 'I sure am glad I left my savings in the other bank that time when you tried to persuade me otherwise. Still, I guess there's a chance the deputy, here, might get the bank funds back again, an' then he'll be up for promotion when old Moses finally retires!'

Sam ignored all the talk. He angled his horse towards the hitch rail in front of the sheriff's office and slid thankfully to the ground. Alongside of the dun was a lean skewbald, which was eating the post because the nearest water trough was just beyond its reach. Sam knew the skewbald. It belonged to Limpy Croat, the town's rather ancient jailer.

He started to call: 'Hey, Limpy, are you in there?'

While he slackened his saddle, his ears caught the sounds of the crippled man hurriedly hobbling across the boards to the office. Limpy's brown seamed face appeared around the door.

'Sure enough, Sam, I'm here. It's good to see you back. Didn't expect to see you this side of noon. What can I do for you?'

'First off, you can lend me this skewbald of yours, because my cayuse is plum tuckered out. An' then you can hop down to the next block an' rustle up a posse by hammerin' on the triangle down there! Think you can do that while I take a look at the scene of the crime?'

The toothless jailor spat upon his hands and at once started off down the boards of the sidewalk. 'Doggone, Sam, twenty years ago I'd have ridden with you, crippled leg or no crippled leg,' he murmured to himself.

Sam, meanwhile, was hurriedly shifting his saddle from one horse's back to the other. He mounted up in the minimum of time and headed off down the street toward the intersection.

The deputy had, indeed, missed the action by barely five minutes. He found the chief cashier sitting in a chair having a skull contusion bathed by the local president, while another of the tellers had suffered a bullet burn across the back of his hand when he attempted to pick up a gun and turn it on the raiders.

The president, who looked shaken, turned and nodded to Sam, and then went back to his patient. He called: 'It's good to see you around, Sam, but you're too late to save the bank's money. I'd say we lost between thirty and forty thousand. Is there any hope of a pursuit?'

Before Sam could reply the distant jangle of the cleaver on the triangle answered the president's query. Sam merely nodded to the injured, and those whose nerves had been shaken. He went out of doors again and began to look around him.

It was clear by the stirring up of the dust where the getaway horses had been placed, prior to the departure. Most men would have been satisfied at that stage, especially after a protracted ride from another town, but Sam could not rest. He studied the surface of the street much closer and paid little attention to the random townsmen who had crept close enough to aim a few bullets at the retiring riders.

'One man on a pinto hoss came away after the others,' a small bandy-legged man said, almost in his ear. 'But he followed the general route of the others, across there, an' to the south, deputy.'

Sam nodded, and thanked his informant. The man had gestured as he spoke, and he had appeared to point towards the alley alongside of the end wall of the composite building. Sam crossed to the alley, not expecting to find anything worthy of note, but he was wrong on this occasion.

One horse had been secreted in the alley, and, judging by its shoe prints, it was one which might be identified again because of a blemish on the outer edge of the left forefoot. The churned up dust was just sufficiently clear to show where the horse had been walked into the passageway. It had then stamped about for a while, and finally been turned around and ridden out again.

Fifteen riders came out of Main Street and reined in at the intersection. Their eyes ranged along the hotel frontage on Main and the bank outer wall which was up the intersection. There was no sign of Sam until he emerged from the alley with a frown of concentration on his face.

Puzzled looks on the faces of the impatient riders pulled his thoughts back to the present. 'All right, boys, glad to have you with me. Jest give me a few seconds to get mounted up and we'll be away.'

Strollers backed out of the way as Sam heaved himself onto the saddle, saluted the bank president and headed the packed group of riders across the intersection and out of town on the south side. They rode at a healthy pace and soon disappeared from view in a rolling cloud of dust.

As Sam rode, his thoughts went back to the words of a man in town. The townsman had said that he, Sam, might recover some of the bank funds, and that if he did, he would be pushing hard to take over the sheriff's job when Moses Wallis retired.

The thought was pleasing. He would like to achieve both objects, but he was in no sort of hurry to take the job of sheriff. It was one thing to be an efficient deputy and another thing to have all the weight for peace keeping throughout a western county.

The skewbald was in good fettle. It kept him slightly ahead of the other riders without too much effort, and for this Sam was glad. He knew the country over which they were riding. He ought to do, seeing that he had spent all his life in the locality. In a shack within a few miles he had been born during the war between the North and South. His father had died as a result of a war wound, and when his mother had later succumbed to a fever, Sam and his older brother and sister had lived on in the same shack, watched by well wishers.

The time had come when the sister married and moved out to Montana, and the older brother had joined the cavalry, the outfit their father had served in. And still Sam had stayed on in the west of Basin County.

The bunched riders were on the trail to Great Wells, south-west of Blackwood and some fifteen miles away. This far the renegades' trail markings had led them, but they would surely turn off somewhere before they reached the lesser town.

A good five miles south of the county seat, a sallow-faced man with a drooping moustache urged his mount to the front of the group and sided Sam. The deputy acknowledged his presence and welcomed it. Jim Siddall was an experienced scout who had once served with the army.

Another mile further along, Siddall

held up his hand and Sam did the same. The whole posse was brought to a prancing halt while the sign was given a closer inspection. Siddall dismounted and did the necessary. He walked slowly back to the side of the deputy and gave his opinion.

'It was here they stopped for a consultation. They split up, Sam. What are you goin' to do, split the posse?'

Sam looked frustrated, but he gave his decision. 'I don't have any alternative. I'd be glad for you men to group yourselves in threes. As soon as you've done that, I'll tell you which direction to ride in. So hurry it up, will you?'

There was a certain amount of argument about the grouping but that was soon resolved. As soon as the shifting horses were separated, Sam, backed by Siddall, pointed out the various directions taken by the outlaws, after they had parted.

One group went westward, heading directly towards the Little Pecos river. Another turned off the trail a little further south. Others went eastward, into the rough unbroken ground between Great Wells and East Halt. A trio went to circle a hogsback ridge, and three more elected to go along with Sam, himself, who had already picked out for himself the most fruitful route to take.

He had noticed that the marked shoe horse had gone off to the south-west in the general direction of sluggish-moving Lesser Creek. This was a place which he had explored for many years until he was old enough to move about and do a man's job.

Lesser Creek was thickly wooded. The outlaw who headed into it probably did not know the area, unless of course he had something special to do near the creek, such as hiding a bag of loot, or something like that.

Left with his own three men, Sam gave them their instructions.

'Boys,' he began, 'with luck we'll be able to flush out one or more outlaw riders from the terrain ahead of us. I want two of you to make for the ford, cross it, and slowly make your way down the other side. Another one should go along the trail for another half a mile, and then turn straight towards the creek. As for me, I'm goin' to follow right in the shoeprints of the man or men we're seekin'.'

'Keep your eyes skinned all the time, an' remember if this jasper has gone to earth, he's dangerous. If you have to shoot, shoot early, an' don't let me have to take any sad messages back to town. Are you ready to go?'

The trio replied in the affirmative, and within half a minute all of them were just about out of sight. Sam took a few deep breaths and started off the track himself. Beyond the trail-side rock the ground vegetation was thick and green. Only occasionally was it possible to detect where a small branch had been broken from a tree by a horse moving quickly.

Soon, he was hearing the dull murmur of the slow-moving waterway, and wondering what manner of man lay ahead of him. Already he had built up a picture of a man who was a little different from the common run of bank robber. This one, for instance, left his horse in an alley, rather than have it in the care of the regular horse minder.

There was a distinct possibility that the horse was a pinto, too, and that he would come face to face with it before the day's venture was over.

Maybe the man who had gone to earth before the almost still waters of the creek was not a stranger, at all.

Sam knew the area. Why should not another man be similarly acquainted with it?

2

Sam made a hundred yards of progress without anything happening. The meandering creek on his right hand was coming steadily closer as he rode, but there were no signs on its banks of anyone having stopped for a breather, or of a hasty crossing. Neither were there any signs of his own men. The pair who had gone to the ford were somewhere to the north of him, while the man who had progressed down trail was that much further south.

The deputy began to upbraid himself. He was allowing the gentle sounds of the water and the sighing of the wind in the scattered trees and thick foliage to blunt his senses.

Somewhere in this prolonged thicket, there very likely was a desperate criminal who would defend his right to live and to be free with every breath he drew.

A quarter of a mile went by, and then Sam's neck hairs began to prickle. Suddenly he felt too conspicuous perched up on the back of the borrowed skewbald. He reacted to his instincts, slipping to the ground and hauling out his Winchester. Thus armed with a shoulder weapon and his .45 Colt, he gave the horse a slap which sent it in the direction of the creek bank. It wanted no encouragement to go and partake of the waters.

Crouching from time to time, Sam found himself moving through the stunted pines with growing caution. He felt sure that the man he sought had gone to earth, and that he was not far away. Progress was slow, with a wide scanning terrain on every side for a man chancing to slip behind him.

For another fifty yards, he walked forward. By that time, the tension in him had so grown that further progress came only with a conscious effort. The spaces between one tree bole and another seemed enormous. He was about to start from behind yet another trunk when a sudden skittering laugh sent a chill down his marrow and made him duck back again.

There was a small clearing ahead, and somewhere just beyond its far boundary there was a thud, as if a body had dropped out of a tree.

The actual bump had little effect upon Sam. He was thinking about the laugh. It had had a signal effect upon him. The laugh itself did not trouble him, except that he had heard it before — or one almost exactly like it.

His mind had slipped back in time a little way. He conjured up a vision of one of his youthful friends, Pete Arnott. In the days when Pete's father, old Arthur Arnott, owned three big liveries in the Creek Basin towns, Pete and Sam had played for hours in these same lush stretches of open country.

Even now, when Mr Arnott had retired, and his family spent most of their time at a house outside Great Wells, Sam and Pete's trails often crossed. The Creek Basin had held them both, although Pete had shown several times in the past five years that he had itchy feet. He had figured in as many small business deals in and around the towns as he had digits upon one hand. Nothing ever seemed to come of them.

Whether he made losses, or not, Sam never knew. If Pete did lose, his father, no doubt, would square up the accounts, because it was well known that Arthur had sold out for a goodly sum, and that he had made a pile of money during the time when he was building up the businesses.

On his edge of the clearing, Sam remained watchful. He had a strong feeling that he was at the wrong end of another man's gun sights. But nothing happened. All had gone quiet since the dull thump reminiscent of a dropping body. Sam licked his dry lips. He wondered if this sudden shooting of his thoughts back to Pete Arnott had any significance or whether he was simply thinking about Pete because of the laugh, and because this was territory which they had played in together.

He could not be sure. After a time, he became restless. He did not want to be in this seemingly foolish position when the rest of the trio backing him happened along. He hefted a stone, and tossed it in the direction of the laugh.

Suddenly and surprisingly the laugh came again. It was more long drawn out this time. How could another man have a laugh exactly similar to Pete Arnott?

Sam cleared his throat: 'Hey, you over there! This is Deputy Sheriff Regan callin' to you! Whoever you are, step out into the clearin' an' keep your hands above your head while you do it! Do you understand?'

Again the laugh, followed by a reply. 'I hear you, deputy, but why be so formal. After all, I guess you know who this is. It ain't as if we're strangers, Sam, is it now?'

'Is that you, Pete? Pete Arnott?'

'Sure it's me, Sam. Who else would it

be in this area we know so well? And why are you stalkin' me, an' usin' your official voice? Answer me that!'

Still no sign of the man dug in on the other side.

'Because I'm on official business, an' it's no game, Pete. Bein' who you are doesn't excuse you! I've got a gun lined up on the spot where you are an' I'm huntin' a man on a pinto hoss for reasons known to most folk in Blackwood, for bank robbery!'

As soon as he shouted this long answer, Sam began to move again. He worked his way slowly round the lower side of the clearing, his straining ears detected the next exchange.

'I know you're movin' up on me, Sam, but I don't figure what you're doin' will do you a whole lot of good. You see, I don't figure to surrender myself to anyone belonging to a posse, an' I can't see you takin' me the hard way!'

'How do you mean, takin' you the hard way?'

Sam knew what he meant all right, but he was playing for time, and hoping against hope that he would not have to use his gun on his old friend.

'I mean you won't shoot the son of a man who helped to put you into the job of deputy to the County Sheriff! It wouldn't be the thing, would it, Sam? Jest think about it, will you?'

The deputy made another ten yards before slowing down. He was thinking a whole lot harder than his quarry gave him credit for. In their boyhood games, Pete had proved that he could be tricky, on occasion. What if he was allowing Sam to walk close so that he would be a sitting duck?

'I'm thinking, amigo. One thing is plain. You haven't once said you're innocent of the affair at the bank. That has to mean something. I can't figure you out any more. Why should you be involved in a shady affair like that? A robbery with pistol whippin' and a teller wounded? Why don't you tell me it's all a mistake? If you're innocent, you've nothing at all to fear!'

After a pause, Pete called back. 'I have a pinto hoss, an' I don't think you'd believe me, even if I did claim to be innocent of a bank robbery, so what's the use? Remember, I've seen you on the hunt before. It's sure different though, bein' the hunted!'

Five yards nearer, Sam said: 'Pete, you're goin' to have to do something positive in the next minute or two, an' if you're bankin' on my not shootin' at you because we happened to be friends before today, think again. Rightly or wrongly, your Pa helped me into my job, but I won't disgrace my office by holdin' back fire when I know that I should shoot! Don't make me do something I don't want to do!

'And if you're a renegade then you ought to be on the run, not holed up here in a spot where boys used to play. There's no future in doin' things the way you are!'

Sam knew sudden anger. He started forward at a faster pace, not taking quite so much care over keeping himself hidden. This move was almost his undoing. A rifle bullet came out of the trees in front of him and to his left. It buzzed by his ear and set his heart palpitating in a most alarming fashion.

He wanted to shout in anger, but for a few moments his voice was denied him. He went to his knees, recovered his balance and started forward again. The time for talking was most obviously over. Pete Arnott had set the seal on their coming clash. Using all his will power, Sam now strove to obliterate from his mind that the man he was stalking had been a friend.

Two minutes later, he had rounded the end of the clearing and he was steadfastly moving up on the spot where the rifle had been fired. If Pete stayed in the same place, then he was a fool. He was inviting retaliation.

A similar period of time elapsed. Sam chose for himself a fairly wide tree bole and slowly straightened up behind it. He was easing his muscles when the next happening occured. This time no less than three bullets were aimed at his tree between chest and head height. He sank down lower for safety's sake, and at the earliest possible moment he took a look around at knee level.

Just as he did so, Pete broke cover. He ran from the trees to the boundary of the glade and started around it. Somewhere on that side, he had left his mount.

Sam knelt. He brought up his Winchester and managed to get the running man in the sights for upwards of five seconds. His first shot missed about shoulder level, but the second was on target. As Pete turned to give a backward glance, prior to darting back into cover, the leaden bullet entered his chest under the right arm and lodged in the region of the heart.

He sank down at once, and Sam broke cover, racing across to where he had fallen. The smoking Winchester grew heavy before the ground was crossed, but it still gave a feeling of security to its owner.

Pete was on his back with one foot tucked under him. He had lost his own rifle, and his hand had been on the way to one of his holsters, but his strength had ebbed first. A spreading patch of blood was welling out from the side of his chest and rapidly staining his grey shirt under the vest of the same colour.

Sam paused, breathless beside him. He went down on one knee and propped Pete's head on his leg. Although Pete was twenty-five now, he had not changed much since he was sixteen or seventeen. His hair was the same short carrotty red, his grey eyes still looked a trifle too close to his long nose, and the blue bandanna which he habitually wore, was knotted carefully at the side of his neck.

Sam thought about getting some water, but Pete read his thoughts and shook his head.

'Why did you do it, Pete? You had everything you wanted! Your Pa would have let you hunt in these woods for the rest of your days, if you'd only behaved yourself. Why did you have to tangle with renegades, in your situation?'

The anguish Sam was feeling came through in his voice. He was a very different character now from the formal peace officer of a few minutes earlier.

Their eyes studied each other. One set showed physical pain and the other mental anguish.

Pete murmured: 'Bein' able to do anything you want all the time gets tedious, Sam. But I must admit I didn't expect to end my days in this neck of the woods. What are you goin' to say to my Pa? He'll hound you out of the office when he knows what you've done. An' then there's Mirabelle. I often thought my sister could do whole lot better than you. Now, maybe, she'll see the light and look elsewhere.'

'But I only see her every now and then, since your Pa moved to the house outside Great Wells,' Sam argued.

He recollected that he was arguing with a dying man, and at once gave up.

In the following minute, Pete became very much more feeble. He was looking out of the corner of his eye, and trying to engage Sam's attention once more, but the tiny bubbles of blood coming from his mouth seemed to indicate that he had spoken his last.

A look of entreaty made Sam put his face closer. Maybe Pete wanted to tell him something really significant before he died, like why he was hanging about in the woodland, rather than putting miles between himself and those who followed after.

Pete made the effort. He said: 'What sort of a story are you goin' to tell my Pa, Sam? How good are you as a story teller?'

The stricken man's eyes rolled almost at once. His head circled on Sam's knee and the life ebbed out of him. All spent at the tender age of twenty-five. Sam lowered the head to the ground and put the hat over the face. He walked about five yards and sat himself down against a tree bole.

Pete was dead, and what would he — Sam — say to the father? Could he say that he had done it in the course of his duty, and then beg for pardon? It would be a singularly difficult thing to do. Arthur Arnott, even since the rodeo injury had left him carrying excess weight, was a formidable man to deal with. He would do all that Pete had forecast, and more, if he knew all the facts about Pete's end. And how would Mirabelle take it? Gentle, lively Mirabelle, who was only twenty years of age that summer. Would she be able to face the knowledge that her brother was a bank robber, that he had been shot while making his escape? What about when *she* knew his friend had killed him with a gun?

Sam groaned. For a short time he wished that he had never become a peace officer. It was too exacting when the law had to be upheld against a man's friend. In his anguish, he was overlooking the fact that the friend was to blame.

And then his brain began to function. Almost everyone who heard that Pete was a renegade would be shocked by disbelief. What if it were possible to concoct a story to make it seem that Pete was an innocent bystander? Was that a possibility? He thought it might be.

After all, Pete was known to have spent a great deal of time in the area where he had died. Why shouldn't he have been there for some purpose of his own? A little fishing, or shooting . . .

★ ★ ★

Ten minutes later, the man who had ridden downtrail before heading into Lesser Creek country came through the underbrush at a good speed. He was a beetle-browed middle-aged livery hand by the name of Burgin, and he had seen the skewbald where Sam had left it.

Soon, Burgin was crossing the clearing, and Sam was building up to

31

tell the big lie to his first contact.

'This here is poor Pete Arnott. He's shot to death, Burgin. Some place around here I'd say you'll find a tired pinto hoss, the one the outlaw came out from town on. I guess the renegade must have shot Pete and taken his hoss to make his getaway on. You see, this pinto has a mark on one of its shoes.'

Burgin's face worked. He did everything barring talk for upwards of half a minute. And then he started.

'But the killer, he can't be far away. Poor Pete is past help now, God rest his soul, but the other hombre can't be too far ahead of us, deputy. How would it be if we leave Pete an' try to corner the jasper before he gets away from Lesser Creek?'

'You've got a good point there, Burgin,' Sam acknowledged. 'You ride forward an' flush him out. Me, I'll look for the pinto, an' make sure he ain't skulkin' around any place. Off you go. Go right ahead, an' remember to get in touch with the other two across the creek if you want help.'

Burgin went. He left Sam sighing with relief that his initial lies had been believed.

3

Having so much on his mind, Sam did not see the pinto as quickly as he might have done. But when he did find it, cropping some grass in a thicket, it was the one he had expected to find, right down to the mark in the shoe of its left forefoot.

He walked it back to the place where Pete's body lay, and, with a special effort, he managed to get the corpse draped across the back. His next move was to walk the pinto back to the spot where he had left the skewbald.

After that, he sat himself down and rolled a smoke with fingers which were rather unsteady. The smoke was half finished when the three men he was waiting for started to come towards him from the south. The pair who had crossed the creek had made another crossing when they thought they had circled the outlaw.

Burgin, a normally silent man, was doing most of the talking when they crossed the open glade and came to a halt beside Sam and the two horses. Ferris and Leggatt, the other two, dismounted and cautiously took a look at the head of Pete Arnott. After a cursory examination, they shook their heads.

Leggatt remarked: 'There'll be trouble in the county seat when we get back with Pete's body. If I ain't mistaken his Pa and Ma, and the daughter are stayin' at one of the hotels, while the women do some shoppin'. I wish things had turned out some other way. Why did young Arnott have to be skulkin' round this neck of the woods, anyways?'

Ferris could not answer this query. He fingered his bristly chin while he asked: 'Deputy, are we goin' after any more of the outlaws, or do we make our way back to Blackwood with the body?'

Sam was slow to answer. 'I figure we'd better break off an' take Pete

Arnott back into town. Too bad you didn't see the hombre who blasted him an' took his horse.'

Suddenly the trio were all talking at once, but the outcome of their conversation was that they, too, regretted having missed the killer.

At a quarter after five o'clock, Sam pushed the pinto up towards the rail outside the funeral parlour on the south side of Main Street. Perry Malone, the outsize Irish undertaker, hurried through the crowd following the four riders and the corpse.

Screwing his big hat more firmly on his head, the fleshy-faced undertaker flapped his black coat to cool himself. As soon as he was on the sidewalk, he made an effort to assume the dignity which his position entailed. He took off his hat revealing a loose lock of very fair hair, and stepped towards the jack-knifed body over the pinto's back.

Burgin remarked: 'You won't like what you see, Perry. That there is young Pete Arnott. He was shot in a thicket near Lesser Creek while we was huntin' a man who rose out of town on a pinto hoss. He's on the pinto right now, but the man who shot him gave us the slip. Must have wanted Pete's hoss is the way we figure it.'

Sam slipped to the ground. 'I'll give you a hand to get him into the parlour.'

Malone looked as though he was going to refuse the offer of help, but Sam insisted, and, soon, with Burgin helping, they removed Pete's body and transferred it to the wooden bench in the back room of the establishment.

'This will shake poor Arthur, Sam. Besides, he's right here in town with his womenfolk. I can't rightly think what I'm goin' to say to him, but somebody ought to seek him out otherwise he's goin' to hear the sad news from somebody gossipin' in the street.'

Sam wandered about, gripping his hat. 'I know it's a difficult message to give to anyone, but I'd be obliged if you'd do it, Perry. You see, it would be even worse for me, and besides, I have to get back to the office an' check on the other members of the posse as they come in.'

The undertaker patted Sam on the shoulder, and undertook to deliver the message. Burgin made himself responsible to see the pinto horse delivered to the livery, and presently Sam found himself out on the street again.

Many people were hanging about doing nothing more searching than just looking at the protagonists in the recent bit of action, but to Sam their eyes probed and hurt. He would have given anything for the events down at Lesser Creek not to have included him. Now, he knew what it was like to be thrust into the full glare of publicity following a calamity.

He grabbed the reins of the skewbald and led it along to his office, where Limpy Croat heard a brief description of the recent events before taking over his horse and retiring to the nearest café for a meal.

Already two groups of three riders had reported in, saying that they had lost the men they had been following. In the next half hour, the other groups came back into town with no better news to offer the desperate deputy. As he saw the last trio to the door, Sam realised that if any outlaw had been taken alive, he would probably have made a statement about Pete being one of the gang.

So that in one way, it was a blessing that no others had been taken at this stage. Otherwise, his deception, his lies about how Pete had met his death, would have been contradicted right at the start.

★   ★   ★

Arthur Arnott, retired master livery-man, was in a saloon quenching his thirst with a couple of old cronies when he heard the first whisper that his son, Pete, was dead. He shooed away the first man to bring him the tidings, because the fellow was a drunk, and Arthur assumed that he was merely after the price of a drink.

Arnott senior looked older than his fifty years. He was a bulky man with a full sunburned face, and a bald head fringed by white hair. His moustache was the same colour. In his retirement, he had taken to wearing grey stores suits and light fawn stetsons. He was dressed in this fashion on this particular day.

Although he gave no credence to the talk put forward by the cadger, Arthur was shaken by the substance of it. He continued to talk to his cronies about horses, and the politics of the day, but at the same time he had started to watch the batwing doors, as though anticipating the arrival of a man with news of a similar nature.

The sight of Perry Malone made him wince. He started to feel in his bones that the drunk's whisper had been the truth. He started limping towards the undertaker, intending to offer him anything in the house in the way of a drink, but his throat dried out, and he simply met the fellow half way to the door and waited for his revelations. Malone gripped him by the shoulder before making his pronouncement.

'There's been an accident, Arthur. The posse rode out in search of the bank robbers, an' they came upon your son, Pete. He must have been involved with one of the robbers after they split up, because he was shot, an' the jasper who did it left behind a pinto hoss known to have come to the bank. I'm sorry. Pete is at my place. If you want to come along right away an' see him, it'll be all right. Maybe you didn't ought to bring the women along yet, though.'

Arthur excused himself. He gripped Malone by the arm and went out with him. At the funeral parlour, he examined his son's remains as though they belonged to another person. He was half-stunned, and yet he knew he had to accept the evidence of Pete's death right there before his eyes. And then there was the matter of breaking the news to Martha and Mirabelle. It wouldn't do for them to hear the tidings from one of the town's drunks.

'I'm goin' now, Perry, to inform my folks. As soon as they've taken a look at him, get down to business. Measure him for a box in the best timber. Make it tomorrow, if you can fix it. Ain't no reason to delay with affairs of this kind. By the way, who brought in the — the body?'

'It was Sam Regan. He went closer than anyone else before the actual shootin'. Maybe you could talk with Sam later. Right now, he's a little upset, as you can understand. I'll start to get the work under way as soon as possible, like you say, Arthur. Tomorrow afternoon will be okay.'

* * *

Arthur Arnott limped into the office of Sheriff Moses Wallis with the colour drained from his face, and his limp seemingly more pronounced than of late. He found Sam Regan in there on his own. Sam came up out of his chair as though he had been catapulted. He advanced to meet his visitor with his hand outstretched.

'Mr Arnott, I sure am sorry about what has happened. It must have come as an awful blow to you. I wish I'd been in town when the strike took place, instead of on the way back from North Creek. That way, things might be different. Will you convey my condolences to Mrs Arnott an' Mirabelle. Sorry I haven't seen them to speak to durin' this visit to town, but you know how it is.'

'Sure, sure, Sam, I know you're busy. I knew you'd have your work cut out when I helped to ease you into the job you have. I hope Moses will soon be fit again, then maybe you'll be able to use your energies to track down this bunch of treacherous renegades.'

At last the hand shaking came to an end. Arnott settled himself briefly on an upright chair, and Sam settled back onto the swivel. The latter was perspiring hard. He was learning how difficult it was to live with a tissue of lies.

'Tell me one thing before I go, Sam. Would a man really kill another for his horse?'

Sam shrugged and lowered his eyes. 'I think a man would, Mr Arnott. An English king was said to have offered his kingdom for a horse after a battle. I don't know whether that was true or not, but this renegade was in a desperate situation. After a robbery, an' with a posse on his tail. Besides, Pete's rifle had been fired three or four times. But you would know the answer to your own question, seein' as you've been in the horse handlin' business for most of your life.'

Arnott started to nod in a rather distant fashion. 'I can't figure which hoss Pete was usin' today. Maybe I've spoiled him. Although I'm out of active business myself he still has the right to take out any hoss in the various

44

establishments I used to own. Still, that's besides the point. I know you'll do what you can to apprehend the killer, Sam. You of all people. And the burial will be tomorrow afternoon, if you can find the time to attend.'

Sam shook hands again, and ushered his unwanted guest out of doors.

★   ★   ★

The short funeral service beside the grave at Boot Hill was well conducted. Most of the town's dignitaries and senior townsmen and women went along to pay their last respects.

Mirabelle Arnott had her lush bell of auburn hair tied back in a black ribbon. She was also wearing a black bonnet and an ankle length dress of the same colour. Martha Arnott, her mother, looked smaller, more stooping and thinner, as Mirabelle supported her. Obviously, the death of her only son had badly shaken her. It would take a long time for poor Martha to revive.

As the concluding words of the service were spoken, Arthur stepped closer to his wife and took her by the arm. When she sagged against him he put his arm round her, and Mirabelle, temporarily relieved, moved a little further away. Having deposited the wreath of flowers which she had been holding, the girl gravitated towards Sam Regan, who was standing a little further back and to one side. Her wide-set green eyes were bright with unshed tears, and yet she wanted to make contact with Sam, for whom she had always felt a warm affection. She moved closer to him and slipped her gloved hand under his arm.

'Sam, ain't all this to do sad? Do you have anything to say to me that could make me feel better?'

She looked into his face, and for a short while the burial ground and the mourners receded. She was seeing only Sam, an old friend. He was bareheaded and clutching his hat. His white bandanna had been discarded in favour of a black one, and a dark tailored jacket topped his brightly coloured shirt.

'I'm not a very good man with words, Mirabelle, but I could take you for a stroll around the burial ground, if you feel so inclined.'

The girl managed a half smile. 'Why, Sam Regan, you never miss an opportunity, not at any time, I do declare.'

This gentle mockery had the effect of making Sam stiffen up as they walked away from the graveside. On the brief stroll, he answered her few questions in monosyllables. It was when they were almost back again that Sam's usual keen interest in life appeared to be reborn.

'Mirabelle, I've been looking over the young men who happened along to the burial. Maybe you know Pete's recent friends better than I do. Take a look at that young hombre restin' his weight on the gate. Do you know him?'

Mirabelle glanced at the young man,

and at once looked away again. She noted that Sam's eyes, the same colour as her own, were looking rather harsh and unfriendly.

'Sam, what are you studyin' faces for on an occasion like this?'

'It's my job, Mirabelle. Don't forget there was an armed robbery here in town only yesterday! Somebody has to take an interest in the strangers who come around here. Do you know the fellow?'

'You think the man or men who shot my brother would come along here to see if he was buried properly, Sam?' Without waiting for an answer, she went on. 'For your information, I think I've seen that young man somewhere, but I can't remember who he is. His name eludes me, too. If I'm wastin' your valuable time, I will now return to my parents, an' let you get on with your appraisal of the strangers. Goodbye, Sam.'

Sam started after her. He then gave up the chase and toyed with his hat.

Any sort of a meeting with a member of the Arnott family was likely to prove difficult. *How could he explain to Mirabelle that he was on the lookout for signs of Pete's fellow riders?*

And yet that was what he had been doing. Unlikely as it seemed, he was keeping a lookout for anyone who took a curious interst in the last rites of one Pete Arnott. At that time, he did not know whether Sheriff Moses Wallis would have approved of his surreptitious sleuthing, or whether he was simply becoming morbid through his own personal guilt.

4

Later that day, Sheriff Moses Wallis returned to his office, and the first thing he wanted was a rundown on the business at the bank, and the details of what had happened afterwards, including the setback to Pete Arnott.

Sam told everything as he had told it before. The sheriff asked other questions, and he answered them all, as truthfully as he could, always bearing in mind the big untruth as to how Pete had died. Moses Wallis was an old friend of Arthur Arnott, and having to explain to him did not make Sam feel any better over the matter.

As soon as he could conveniently do so, he asked permission to do some more interviewing. After enquiring about the men to be interviewed the fifty-six year old sheriff gave his approval, and paced his office massaging his back and poking his fierce blue eyes into everything.

When he was well, Wallis was a force to be wary of, and he was almost well now. Soon, he had paused in front of a wall mirror with his scissors in his hand. He went to work on his grey goatee beard with steady practised hands, and that meant for sure that he was back in harness.

In any other circumstances than these, Sam would have been pleased. As it was, he felt that he would never be at ease with his job or his conscience ever again.

He walked the streets and had purposeful conversations with Jake Rimmer, the manager of the Holborn Hotel where the strike had been, and the bank manager, whose domain was an entirely separate business entity.

Sam felt that it was good to be kept busy, but his interviewing did not take him any nearer to solving the strike against the bank. Men were beginning to refer to the outfit which had done the raiding as the Creek Basin Gang, and that title seemed to be as fitting as any other.

In recent years the Creek Basin had not been plagued by outlaw gangs of any significance. Now, it seemed, the situation had changed. Without wanting to appear a pessimist, Sam kept putting forward the theory that the strike against the Bankers' Hotel was probably the first of many.

★ ★ ★

Very late that night, Lester Janes, the town marshal, returned from his visit across the Little Pecos, and a little after eight o'clock the following morning, Sam made over the details as he knew them once again.

Janes was a tall, big-boned man with widely-spaced teeth and hollow cheeks. He looked about as cheerful as Sam Regan felt.

He summed up: 'So the loot has vanished, and all the raiders who took part in the action have gone to earth without trace. Is that a fair summing up, Sam?'

'That's about the size of it, Lester,' Sam said, as he paced the other's office. 'I believe that this county will suffer again from the attentions of the group known as the Creek Basin Gang, but that's a headache for the sheriff, not you. It ain't likely that they will strike in the same place twice, is it?'

Janes shook his head, and he was pleased, in a way, that he had been out of town when the successful strike against the bank had been made. He would have experienced a whole lot more adverse criticism if he had been in town and back on duty at the time.

After a good half hour of talk, Sam's restlessness took him towards the door. He had not said anything definite, but Janes knew he wanted to be on his way. The marshal grinned as Sam came to a halt by the door and casually pointed to it.

'Okay, Sam, so go ahead. You've

given me all the details, but I'd be a fool if I thought the sheriff's office was quietly droppin' this case, as of now. So, if there's anything at all I can do by the way of co-operation from here on in, I know you won't hesitate to ask. Adios, amigo.'

Sam turned back, grinned, adjusted the trim of his hat, and stepped out into the street. It occurred to him as he emerged into the open air that he was getting used to his chronic feeling of uneasiness which had assailed him since the shooting. A man, so it seemed, could adjust to almost anything.

Five minutes later, he was bellied up to the Short Bar in the back of the Bankers' Hotel with a beer in front of him. He did not feel particularly thirsty, but he had come to the hotel in the hope of seeing Mirabelle. His exchanges with her at the cemetery had been so feeble that he did not even know if the Arnotts were staying at the Bankers' Hotel, or at the Lone Star, near the other end of the street.

His beer was half drunk when a familiar figure entered the bar through the communicating door with the dining room. This was the young man who had interested him while leaning against the gate on Boot Hill. The stranger who had come along to the funeral. Sam's interest quickened, but the fellow had spotted him. While the peace officer worked hard to drain his glass, the other man put a match to his small cigar and turned on his heel, going out by the same door.

Sam grounded his glass. He nodded to the barman and followed the newcomer through the door into the dining room. He was just leaving by the foyer entrance. Trailing cigar smoke eddied behind him. Sam slowed his pace, as several tables were occupied, but he went on after the young man who had so intrigued him.

He emerged into the street and saw that his quarry was some forty yards ahead of him, walking briskly up the sidewalk. On the previous day, the fellow had worn a black suit for the burial. Now, with his black sideburns freshly trimmed, he was decked out in a maroon vest, a dark coat and a stetson and trousers of the same shade of grey. A single holstered Colt swung close to his right thigh.

Bunched talkers around the town centre made Sam lose track of his quarry, but one thing was for sure. He was not keen to talk with the deputy.

Sam tried a saloon, and failed to see him because he was seated at a table with a newspaper opened out in front of him. Ten minutes later, he ran the man to earth in the saloon bar of the Lone Star, and this time there was little chance of a withdrawal without talk.

Sam threw out his chest and denied the other the chance to walk by him. Two other early drinkers withdrew about the same time, and the barman, having drawn beer, withdrew from sight on some errand or other. This bar was situated similarly to the Short Bar of the Bankers' Hotel. The dining room was next door. A cursory glance in that direction, however, seemed to show that the next room was empty.

Sam nodded to the only occupant of the bar. 'Howdy, mister, my name is Sam Regan. I'm the deputy sheriff of this area. I'd be glad if you'd spare me a minute or two of your valuable time. I must say you've been harin' around in the past ten minutes. You're workin' up a thirst, maybe?'

The other man shrugged gently. 'In this part of the world, deputy, a man does not have to work to produce a thirst. You've been followin' me quite purposefully, an' I don't suppose I shall get any peace from you until your curiosity is satisfied. My name is Walter Lestrange. What do I have to do for you?'

Sam sipped his beer. 'Your answer is forthright, if not friendly, Mr Lestrange. I wanted to ask you what your interest was in the Arnott family. I saw you at the funeral.'

The stranger raised finely arched

brows. His age was on the right side of thirty. His skin was a good colour.

'Does a man have to have a special interest to honour the dead? Pete Arnott's family is known to my own. Moreover, I have an interest in the Bankers' Hotel, but not the kind of interest which wants to see it robbed.'

'Which of the Creek Basin towns is your home in, Mr Lestrange?'

'South Creek, the southernmost in the locality. But you're wastin' your time with me, deputy. I'm not the man you say shot Pete Arnott down Lesser Creek way. I have other interests. I don't go shootin' young men for their horses.'

Sam cleared his throat. 'Now, see here, Lestrange, nobody is accusin' you of any criminal act. All you're asked to do is answer a few questions. I find your tone an' the way you have of answering rather offensive. What did you mean when you said I'm puttin' it about the way Pete Arnott was shot?'

Lestrange chuckled without humour.

'I don't have to like your questions, Regan, or the way you put them. You're edgy. You have been ever since you came back to town. In fact, you couldn't be more edgy if you had shot Pete Arnott yourself!'

Lestrange had turned to face him. There was a mocking smile on his face as he made this statement. Sam flinched. The barman had returned, and two ranchers, talking and fresh from the street, had entered the bar. Sam forced himself to keep his voice on a conversational tone.

'As far as I'm concerned, Mr Lestrange, that about does it. The way this conversation has gone, I'll have to ask you to step outside to finish it. I take it you'll have no objection?'

Lestrange banged down his beer mug with the dregs still in it. He turned about and left the bar by a door which led into the alley. He had truly divined Sam's proper intent. Both of them wanted the alley. From being an informal questioning, this business between them had turned into a personal thing which could only be settled in one way.

Walter Lestrange said as much as he landed a punch on the side of Sam's head, almost before the door had finished closing behind them.

Sam gasped and backed away from a straight right hander delivered into his chest. Lestrange had the makings of an amateur boxer. He moved well, and for upwards of three minutes Sam was mostly on the receiving end of two fists which moved with educated precision. It was only when Lestrange began to breath a little more heavily that Sam got on terms, and began to throw punches himself.

At first his punches were blocked, or avoided by clever footwork, but soon, when he tried feinting, he began to get through to the handsome fellow's head and chest. By the time he began to have the better of the exchanges, both their hats had sailed off and Lestrange had a slight trickle of blood coming from one nostril.

Lestrange tried trading punch for punch, but Sam had a slight weight advantage, and he was in better trim. Three solid haymakers in succession finally went through Lestrange's guard. Two hit in the chest, and the third fell squarely along the angle of his jaw.

He sank to the ground, and his eyes fluttered, prior to closing. Sam stepped back, having had enough. He knew that he had allowed himself to be provoked very easily into fistic action, and what he had done would scarcely find favour with Moses Wallis, should Lestrange choose to voice the matter around town.

Sam turned his back on him. He wiped his blotchy face on his white bandanna, and walked out of the alley, hoping that his recent bout of fisticuffs was not too obvious in his appearance. As he crossed the foyer, he met the one person he no longer wanted to meet; Mirabelle.

She came out wearing a flat-crowned

stetson, a cream shirt and a grey half-skirt for riding. Her arm linked through his. She said: 'I'm jest goin' for a short ride in a buckboard. Come with me. Pa says I ought to do it to take me out of myself. You will come with me, won't you, because there's things I want to say to you.'

The girl was so full of enthusiasm for the ride, and for his company that Sam could not refuse. He gave in with a good grace, and a few moments later was mounting up beside her on the buckboard outside the livery.

Mirabelle insisted that he should take the reins. As they left town, she began to open up a little.

'Sam, I think it was magnificent the way you punched that fellow, Lestrange. Nobody could ever accuse you of hidin' behind your badge of office. He deserved it, after the way he almost accused you of shooting my brother. Didn't he?'

The girl was moving affectionately towards him, but Sam felt as though he was being torn in two. He turned towards her and asked the obvious question.

'How did you know he said that? Did he talk to you?'

'No, I came down from my room a short while ago, an' I happened to overhear part of your conversation from the dining room. When I knew what was goin' to happen, I kept quiet and went back upstairs for a while. I'm glad you stood up to him like you did Sam. Dear old dependable Sam. In his lifetime, Pete often used to refer to you as 'Good old dependable Sam,' but I know how important it is to have a man about the place who is dependable, so don't think we used to mock you.'

Sam knew that he should have been visibly warming to these overtures from Mirabelle, but how could he when he knew the reason why he had fought with Lestrange was his own guilty conscience. He kept replying to Mirabelle's small talk with cool, brief answers which added little to the conversation.

After a time, she showed some concern about him, thinking that he had taken a worse beating in the alley than he wanted her to know about. As an 'outing' for two young people of opposite sexes, the ride on the buckboard was unfortunately a failure.

5

In his room at the Lone Star — the one he shared with his wife — Arthur Arnott put the comb through his fine white hair and then transferred it to his moustache. It was eleven o'clock in the morning. Martha was not with him. He was preparing himself to go out on the town to spend a harmless hour or two with one or two cronies he had known for half a lifetime.

Presently he stepped back from the wall mirror and fastened the lower buttons of his vest, donning his jacket and reaching for his hat. When the latter was resting on his head at a jaunty angle, he was ready to go. He extracted a cigar from the breast pocket of his coat and lit it from a match, which he struck on the sole of his boot.

At last, he was on his way. He stepped to the door, opened it and made his way to the staircase. He walked quietly, so that his wife, who was visiting down the corridor, did not know he was leaving. That way, he did not have to explain where he was going, who he was going to see, or what time he would be back.

He descended the stairs to the foyer, favouring his better leg and was about to cross the floor to the front entrance, when the middle-aged female receptionist cleared her throat and called out to him.

'Oh, Mr Arnott, I sure am glad to catch you before you got out. You see, there's this letter here waitin' for you, an' it might have been urgent. So if you'll be good enough to take delivery of it right now, I'll feel better about it.'

Arnott froze an expression of studied politeness on his face. He moved across to the counter and there received into his hand a letter in an envelope which had on the outside the name of the rival hotel, the Bankers' Hotel.

Arthur held it at some little distance

from his face, stared at it with long-sighted eyes, and grudgingly thanked the woman for her solitude on his behalf.

'Mighty kind of you, ma'am, to go to so much trouble on my behalf. I don't know anyone at the other hotel who would want to write me a letter, but, as you say, it could be urgent.'

The woman gushed, but she was prevented from detaining him any further by the timely arrival of a client from the upper floor back. Arnott hesitated. Eventually, he decided to avail himself of a seat on the settee at the far side of the foyer. He would read the letter first, and then go out to meet his cronies. He thought that perhaps it would show a lack of respect if he hurried to a drinking session the day after his son was buried.

He ripped open the envelope and stared down at the single sheet of Bankers' Hotel notepaper which was folded across inside it. There was no inside address, but the writer had put his — the recipient's — name at the head of it.

Arthur Arnott Esq.,
The Lone Star Hotel.

Dear Mr Arnott,

I find certain considerations relating to your son's death rather intriguing. Perhaps you ought to bear them in mind yourself, as I am sure you are keen to know the full truth about your son's sad end.

Do you find it strange that no one saw the outlaw who had shot your son and taken his horse? Has it ever occurred to you that the outlaw in question might never have been near your son, that he could have been a figment of another man's imagination?

Deputy Sam Regan was on the spot. He could have been the one to shoot Pete, himself. Don't forget he had the law on his side. He said he had followed a marked shoe print all the way from town, and that the pinto was the horse with the give-away print.

What if that pinto was Pete's horse all the time, and his old buddy, the deputy sheriff, shot him down, knowing he had helped to rob the bank?

If you think this theory holds water, why don't you question the deputy sheriff a little further. After all, there are many people who deserve to be told the truth.

(Signed)   A well wisher.

As he read through the message, Arnott's face went grey and pasty looking. Here was a suggestion to which he had not given any credence. Sam Regan had pursued Pete, and shot him down? Was it really possible, or was the writer of the letter a poison-pen letter writer, a raker up of trouble?

Arnott felt his age, as he sat back on the settee, and contemplated the awful possibilities outlined in the letter. His heart thumped and he felt a slight pain in his left upper arm. What sort of a man could shoot down his own boyhood friend, and then pass his death off as the handiwork of another?

Surely not Sam Regan? How could Sam do such a thing? He and Pete had hunted along the banks of the Lesser Creek, practised with their first firearms in that same location. Surely Sam could not do such a thing! And yet Sam took his duty very seriously. He might have done it if he thought the man he was aiming at was a renegade.

But how could he mistake Pete for a renegade? Pete wouldn't be fool enough to mix with men who would rob a bank. Sam would know that. And yet the accusations in the letter needed more explanation. Perhaps if Sam were asked for more details by an independent person . . . Arthur did not feel as if he could ask such questions himself.

After all, Sam was Pete's buddy. A friend of the family, too. It would not do for Arthur to ask him questions which expressed grave doubts as to his integrity. This was a job for the sheriff, Moses Wallis.

★ ★ ★

At eleven thirty that morning, Sheriff Moses Wallis was dealing efficiently with two informational queries put to him by a pair of visiting salesmen. He sent one of them to a specific establishment and recommended the other to make contact with a high class shop in South Creek.

He was just ushering the pair to the door, watched in an admiring fashion by Limpy Croat, when Arthur Arnott knocked briefly and admitted himself. There was something about Arthur's manner which suggested at once that something had happened since the funeral.

Moses finished dismissing his visitors, and then he sent Limpy out on a message which could have been done at any time of the day on any day of that week. As soon as they were alone, Moses pulled his best visitor's chair towards his desk and requested Arthur to occupy it.

Moses remarked, when he had seated himself: 'Arthur, I can see that something's happened. I sent Limpy out because it looked as if you wanted a confidential chat. Am I right?'

Arthur nodded, and forced a smile. 'You sure are right, old friend. And I don't know another place throughout the Creek Basin where I'd get better co-operation.' He slowed up, and patted the pocket which held the letter. 'Moses, a certain letter came into my possession a short while ago. It deliberately set my mind along a different track connected with Pete's death. Can you possibly visualize a situation, *the* situation with no elusive renegade to take pot shots at Pete?'

Wallis frowned. He fingered the edge of his grey goatee as though checking on the way it was growing. 'Arthur, I have to admit that your words puzzle me. The bullet that killed Pete had to come from somewhere. That much we have to allow for. Now, what was it you were tryin' to say?'

Arnott's mouth worked with no words coming. He pushed a hand inside his jacket and produced the letter, now slightly crumpled.

'Here, you'd better read this for yourself. Then you'll see why I don't find it easy to make sense.'

Wallis frowned again, but he took the letter, extracted it from its envelope and spread it out on his desk to peruse it. He seemed to take an age to read it, and, in fact, he had read it twice before he raised his eyes and glanced at his old friend's perspiring face.

'I can see now why you're rattled, Arthur. You think Sam might have shot your Pete.'

The sheriff spoke quietly, and without any signs of conviction. He might have been talking to the walls of his office. After what seemed like a really long delay, he remarked: 'What has happened has happened, and that's for sure. Sam Regan is a clever, resourceful and competent peace officer. He wouldn't take shots at a man unless he was sure that the fellow was guilty of something.'

Arnott's eyes popped. 'Are you then entertainin' the idea that Pete might have been implicated in the affair at the bank, and that Sam shot him?'

'Isn't that what you're askin' me to do, Arthur, bringin' in a letter like that, which is unsigned? I'll have a talk to Sam again about what happened at Lesser Creek. One thing I can be sure of, an' that is he will not lie in the face of direct questionin'. He's my cousin's son, an' I have a great deal of faith in him, an' still will have that faith when the next interview with him is ended.'

Wallis nodded very decidedly and Arnott, who had not felt particularly belligerent this far, began to get angry. 'The son of your cousin he may be, but when you an' I an' one or two others eased him into the job of deputy sheriff, we didn't see him as shootin' at our own flesh an' blood, an' causin' their deaths, did we?'

The sheriff observed the rising colour in his friend's face. He dipped into a drawer of his desk and produced from it two small cigars. One, he handed over to his visitor, and the other he lit up for himself. Suddenly Wallis was hoping that Sam would not arrive at the office while this interview was going on. Whatever Sam had done or not done, there was bound to be said a whole lot of damaging things which ought to be left unsaid.

When the cigar smoke was effectively calming the atmosphere, Wallis made an attempt to smooth things over. 'I won't ask you if you've checked up on whether that pinto really belonged to Pete, Arthur. You'll have to leave me to interview my own deputy myself, unimpeded, even by you. When I've talked to him, I'll get in touch. How will that be?'

Slowly and with some show of

reluctance, Arthur Arnott rose to his feet. He walked to the window, glanced through it and turned to his old friend.

'All right, Moses. You talk to him. For the time being, I won't tell the womenfolk anythin' about this letter. I'll wait until I've seen you again. But bear this in mind. If you did find out that Sam shot Pete, this is not the end of the matter between us. He'd better have proof of Pete's complicity that will stand up in any court in the land!

'And even then, I shall not be satisfied. No deputy helped into the office will retain his office through me, not when he's been personally responsible for the death of my son. I shall do my damnedest to see Sam relieved of his post, Moses, even though he is the son of your cousin!'

Wallis came over to the door, patted his friend on the shoulder and eased him out into the open air. He did not show one way or the other what he thought about the possible outcome of his next interview with his deputy.

About a half hour after midday, Sam finally showed up at the office. He had not eaten his midday meal, nor did he feel particularly hungry. One look into Moses Wallis' brooding face made him see that something was radically wrong.

'I'm sorry I was away for so long, Moses. I did a few interviews an' then I got caught up with Mirabelle. It sure is difficult to duck invitations from the likes of her, especially when her brother's jest been buried an' her Pa has told her to go out an' look for some sort of distraction.'

Sam turned an upright chair about and straddled it.

'Did she find her distractions, Sam?' the sheriff asked, in a rather hollow voice.

'I don't think I was particularly good company for her, but you must have something on your mind. Something more pressin' than whether Mirabelle is bearin' up or not.'

'You're right, Sam, I have. Arthur has received a letter which suggests exactly how his son might have died. I have to ask you right out. Did you kill Pete Arnott?'

'Yes, I did.'

The confession was out before Sam took time to think about it, and even the simple statement in three words to his superior made him feel a tiny bit better about the whole unsavoury business.

'You want the whole story, Moses?'

'Nothing less than the whole story will suffice between us two, Sam, especially when another story has been put around!'

There was a note of protest in his voice when Sam remarked: 'Do you think Arthur could stand for everyone to know that his only son is an outlaw, or was an outlaw, Moses?'

Before the sheriff could answer, Sam launched into his narrative. He told how he had arrived back in town, dashed to the scene of the crime and found the hoofprints of the pinto horse with the distinctive mark on its left forefoot. How he had formed up the posse, chased the outlaw bunch down the Great Wells trail, and then split them up when the outlaws parted.

About the shooting at him from the terrain on the side of Lesser Creek, he went into great detail; about the first shot, the distinctive laughter, and the verbal exchange between Pete and himself. How Pete had taunted him, saying he would not dare shoot at his old comrade, and so on, and how he had insisted that he would carry out his duty, particularly as Pete would not deny his connection with the pinto with the marked shoe, and where the pinto had been so recently.

'Pete blasted me three times, Moses, an' then broke cover. I fired twice an' hit him with the second shot. He died pointin' out how his Pa would roast me for carryin' out my duty. I never wanted to shoot him an' I told him so quite clearly. I was on the spot, an' I *had* to do it. I believe you would have done the same in similar circumstances.'

Moses hunched in his chair and shrugged away from this counter claim by his deputy. After a pause, he said: 'If it's any consolation to you, I believe every word you've said, Sam. But that'll be poor solace for Arthur, when I tell him. I can't avoid that, an' he'll certainly try to have you thrown out of office, 'cause he's in a difficult mood.'

Sam groaned out loud. 'I never did expect to get much relief out of this interview, Moses, but I can tell you it helps to have you believe me. One of these days we'll get very definite proof that Pete was implicated with that bank robbery, but jest when the proof will turn up is anybody's guess.'

The sheriff nodded. 'I know Arthur Arnott better than you think. He'll want his very definite proof of Pete's complicity in the shortest possible time. Arthur ain't goin' to be friendly to either of us, Sam, not in the near future. This office sure has to get things movin'. But where do we start?'

Sam said: 'I'd like to see the letter you spoke about earlier.'

6

One thing Sam was clear about, after a careful perusal of the 'well wisher's' letter. Whoever it was happened to be a pretty shrewd guesser, or else he had some working knowledge of the way the crime had been carried out. But no member of the gang would be fool enough to write a letter which might be traced to him on Bankers' Hotel notepaper.

Sam was frankly puzzled. When Sheriff Wallis came back from interviewing Arthur Arnott towards three o'clock that afternoon, the younger man's brow was furrowed. Only the sheriff's specific instructions about staying in the office had prevented him from going off straight away to the Banker's Hotel in the hope of identifying the writer of the letter.

Sam rose to his feet, saw the troubled

look on Moses' brow, and rested his hip against the desk. 'It was a difficult interview, Moses?'

Wallis crossed to the window and stood scratching his neck behind the beard. 'That's puttin' it mildly, young fellow. At this moment, Arthur would like to have you run out of town, except that he knows such a move would be against the law. So what are we doin' about the letter, and how do we keep an irate father offen your back?'

Sam pointed at his superior. 'First off, I keep out of the way an' I stay busy. I want to investigate the sender of this letter first. Then I want your permission to ride far an' wide in an effort to establish a proper connection between Pete Arnott an' the men who robbed the bank.'

'So long as you don't forget that this office would like to apprehend said renegades an' have them all behind bars with the minimum of time delay,' Wallis reminded him. 'Arnott said I was to tell you not to rest till you've proved the connection between Pete and you know who, an' to make the investigation a short one, but I guess I don't have to labour the way Arthur is feelin'.'

'I really do believe that Arthur will use his influence to have you removed from your job an' sent out of town if you don't come up with the right sort of evidence, an' that pretty soon, too.'

Sam removed his hat and polished the sweatband with his bandanna. He was feeling bitter, and he did not mind his superior knowing it.

'Havin' a renegade for a son sure does make a man lose his sense of proportion, Moses. I wouldn't like to be in Arthur Arnott's shoes, or boots, whichever he wears.'

Wallis made a non-committal noise in his throat. 'Jest remember that this office would also like more concrete evidence that Pete was actin' on the wrong side of the law. I remember sayin' I believed you, but that was a personal thing. Get the evidence for us, Sam, whatever you do, or we might both have to suffer for the lack of it.

'Take as much time as you like, and make your investigations bear fruit. If you have luck on your side, maybe the Creek Basin towns won't have to suffer a series of raids like the one we've jest had. I hope not, anyways.'

Having said his piece, the sheriff was anxious for Sam to get on with the investigation. He dismissed Sam after a brief enquiry as to whether he was all right for funds.

★   ★   ★

Jake Rimmer, the manager of the Holborn Hotel in Blackwood (known as the Bankers' hotel) was a rather flabby individual in his late forties. He had a full face, and fleshy lips, with grey hair brushed across a balding skull. His excess weight made him breathe rather gustily when talking. He was modestly dressed in a tailored grey business suit.

At three-fifteen that afternoon, he was surprised to see Sam Regan arrive at the door of his office with his hat in his hand. Nevertheless, he at once extended a cordial welcome.

'Come in, Sam, do come in. Put your feet up if you feel so inclined. You must be busy, even though the business about the bank strike seems to have gone quiet.'

Sam sat down. He answered the query politely and then came to the point. 'Mr Rimmer, what I have come about must remain a secret from the general public, at least for a while. It may have a bearing on the bank raid, and then it might not. In any case, I'm involved an' I'm makin' an investigation. My findings might very well lead me into the realm of outlaws.'

He produced the letter which had been written to Arthur Arnott and waited for the hotel manager to hook on his spectacles. This, Rimmer did. He read avidly, and with a growing frown upon his face, until he came to the end.

'This — this is a very serious accusation, but why have you brought it to me, Sam? Surely you don't think I wrote it?'

'No, I didn't think that at all, but the notepaper and envelope came from this hotel, and I thought you might be able to help me trace the writer. What do you think? Is it anyone you know?'

Rimmer glanced at him over the top of his spectacles, then returned his gaze to the letter. 'I have a feelin' I've seen it somewhere before. These loops are bigger than most people make them. But I don't think it was written by any regular member of my staff. Where does that take us?'

'What about your visitors? There might be a well wisher among them. Do you have samples of their handwriting?'

'Not as a regular rule, except for the hotel register. Now there's a possibility. If you'll wait a minute I'll go along and fetch it from the foyer.'

Rimmer went and returned in two minutes. He opened the register at the current page and ran his finger down it with Sam looking over his shoulder.

There were about twenty entries down the page, but the writing with the distinctive loops was easy to pick out.

Sam whistled in mild surprise when he saw the name and details.

He read out: 'Walter Lestrange, wine salesman. Home town, South Creek. Forwarding address, Holborn Hotel, Great Wells. So it's a man I've already met. Can you tell me when he left? He appears to have checked out.'

Rimmer was nodding: 'He went along to the telegraph office and booked a room in the Holborn Hotel, the one at Great Wells. Then he came back and packed his things and moved out almost immediately. It was not so long ago. Some time earlier this afternoon.'

'But there's no stagecoach going to Great Wells this afternoon,' Sam pointed out. 'How then did he travel?'

'He rode on horseback, and judgin' by the way he departed he had something on his mind. Perhaps this letter had something to do with it.'

Sam nodded, but he did not throw any more light on the matter. Instead he had another question to ask. 'Did Lestrange attempt to sell you any wine?'

'When he first arrived here, he went through the motions of tryin' to interest me on one or two new lines, but I put him off. He has the right, through the old Holborn regulations, to inspect our wine cellar. He did that, but found that our existing stocks were adequate for some time to come. So he left without any new orders.'

Sam went very thoughtful about this revealing answer to his question. Presently, he smiled and stood up.

'You've been most helpful, Mr Rimmer. For that I'm grateful. Now, I want to clear out in a hurry. I think it is necessary to make personal contact with our friend, Walter Lestrange, although I have talked to him before. I'll be in touch with you again when I get back to town. So for now, adios.'

Rimmer returned the farewell greeting, confirmed his promise not to mention what had passed between them, and showed him to the door.

★ ★ ★

The dun quarter horse soon showed that it was in good fettle as it settled down on the trail to Great Wells, but Sam rode it with mixed feelings as it carried him towards the area where the posse had dispersed in the fateful day of Pete Arnott's death.

His thoughts impinged upon the fatal clash near Lesser Creek, and he fervently wished that the happenings had not taken place. If only the dun had flagged on the way into town from North Creek, or something happened to deter him from getting the posse on the trail so soon after the bank raid had occurred. He sighed, knowing it was of no use to hope for different circumstances.

As the hours of late afternoon sped by, and the miles of trail were steadily covered, his thoughts turned once again to Walter Lestrange. Had he done a wise thing in following a man who had riled him by hitting upon the truth?

Could Lestrange be some sort of a front man for the outlaw gang, or was it merely a coincidence that he had happened to be at the Bankers' Hotel at the same time as the bank had been raided? Was he travelling many miles with only a slim chance of getting further information about the bank raid, and about Pete Arnott's connection with the gang?

Had Lestrange's hitting upon the truth about Pete Arnott's death been merely inspired guesswork, or had the wine salesman some special knowledge about the goings on of that day which had prompted him to arrive at the truth? He had claimed to know something of the Arnott family, sufficient to have him attend the funeral. Did he, in fact, know anything of the link between Pete and the bank raiders?

Did Lestrange have an ulterior motive in being at the Bankers' Hotel?

The hour had advanced towards seven in the evening by the time his troubled thoughts began to clear. Lesser Creek had started to meander away towards the west, and the ridge which had figured in the abortive pursuit had fallen behind.

Timber stands appeared on either side of the trail in staggered lines. To eastward at a distance of over a mile, he began to catch glimpses of the upper part of another ridge, one which was in the shape of a crescent. Dwarf pines covered the upper slopes like green fur on the back of some great squatting prehistoric beast.

Sam fed his imagination on the distant landmark and knew some mental relief. A side-trail, off to the east, started at a rutted fork, curving towards the crescent ridge and running in the general direction of East Halt, another of the Creek Basin towns south-east of Blackwood, the county seat.

This lesser trail was infrequently

used, and, therefore, to some extent grown over with weeds. There was a thin pall of dust hanging about the area of the fork, but Sam could not visualize Walter Lestrange taking to the lesser track after he had booked in at Great Wells.

The sudden flurry of gunfire from the direction of the crescent occurred about five minutes after the secondary route had gone by.

Sam pulled up sharply, once again aware of the vastness of the country in which he lived. Along the trail which led to East Halt a clash was occurring. Instinct told him that the gunfire had nothing to do with the ordinary everyday hunting of animals.

After a short pause, the tug of duty made him backtrack to the fork and take the other route. He felt a queasy feeling in the stomach as he anticipated trouble.

7

The whole area of the ridge was reverberating with the swelling echoes of gun shots as the dun hurtled along the lesser trail towards trouble. It was a long mile to the crescent sprawl of rock, and every few minutes shoulder weapons sounded off directly ahead.

In the last furlong the dun began to slacken its pace. Its muzzle was foam-flecked and Sam knew that it had done well after the protracted ride from Blackwood. Ahead of him the firing had become more spasmodic. He began to wonder if it would die out altogether before he came within striking distance. And what would that mean?

Very probably he would arrive to find a dead body, or bodies, beside the trail, and a burial job to be done before the buzzards of the area had time to get busy with their beaks and talons. Sam thought that he had seen enough of the seamy side of his job to last him a long time. He hoped that he would arrive in time to take a hand, and that the right would prevail against the wrong, whatever was happening.

He came round a bend and saw the first signs of what was happening ahead of him. The 'rump' of the ridge was bulking above him and to the north, and to one side of it a single man with a smoking rifle was contemplating making a move which would take him down to trail level.

Sam reined in and took the dun a little to one side. He watched the fellow up on the rock. The rifleman had a commanding view of the trail down in front of the ridge. He was looking for the best opportunity to drop to trail level and cross the track.

A quick scrutiny through a spyglass suggested that the opposition was hunkered down amid the rocks opposite to the ridge on the south side of the trail. Most of the shooting was coming from trail-side rocks on the north side. An ambush had taken place just a short while earlier. Whoever was being ambushed was holding on rather grimly against several other guns ranged up in the rocks opposite him.

This far, the man in trouble had given a fairly good account of himself, but any time now, the man on the high rock would drop down to trail level and scamper across the track to try and get behind him. The ambushed man was about to be surrounded, and the gunman on the rock was a key figure in the strategy.

Sam urged the dun closer. He rode for nearly a hundred yards with the marksman in view still hesitating to make his move. Sam dared not wait longer. He checked his mount, slipped to the ground and hauled his Winchester out of the scabbard. He ran five yards to a flat rock which was sticking out of the ground a foot or so. It was a good platform on which to take aim.

With the Winchester at his shoulder,

he concentrated his aim on the gunman's upper trunk. The man was moving a little, as though preparing himself to leap. If Sam was going to fire at him before he dropped out of sight, the job would have to be done quickly.

Three, four seconds more went by. Then the deputy squeezed his trigger and felt the recoil against his shoulder. His aim was good. His victim was hit somewhere around the shoulder. The fellow slowly toppled over, with the face mask which had concealed his features gently fluttering in the light breeze.

The body folded across the outer edge of the rock and then dropped, with a little movement of the limbs. It fell out of sight, and while the shot was still echoing around the area, Sam took his chance to move in closer.

There was a lull of over a minute after the spectacular and unexpected removal of the man on the rock. Ambushers and ambushed must have been surprised. Then two shots came from the ambushed man. He was trying out the resolution of the rest of his attackers, after one of their number had been removed by an unexpected arrival.

At least three guns fired back at him, and it appeared that the fight was still to go on. By this time, Sam was truly keen to be further involved. He ran with his Winchester until he achieved a small talus slope of rocks which led up to the one where his victim had been.

Slowly, and with great care he began to climb. The heels of his riding boots slipped every now and then on the uneven surfaces of the mossy rocks, but he kept his feet and within three minutes he was bellied down on the flat top of the key rock with his weapon beside him.

Another minute went by before his breathing started to improve. Then he was easing himself forward, using his toes and knees towards a rim of the rock which would give him a glimpse of what was going on beyond. Just as he started to raise his head, there was a flurry of shooting from the rocks in front of the crescent. All of them were aimed at another cluster on the south side of the trail.

Seconds elapsed and then a single rifle shot was fired back. It was homed on a rock, but did not do any harm. There was a lot of argument going on among the rocks, as though the ambushers were trying to make up their minds to form a new plan of action. Sam saw an occasional masked head bobbing about, but he had no clear view for careful shooting. As the situation still appeared to be critical, he decided to do what he could to dissuade the attackers.

If he couldn't manage straight shooting, then he would have to put in one or two ricochets.

The barrel of his gun wagged through a small arc until he had decided exactly which rocks to aim at. Hatless, he waited another brief period of time, and then squeezed again. No sooner was his first bullet away than he was levering and firing again.

Altogether he fired four shots. Twice he heard sharp cries from the direction of the attackers, but he could not tell for sure whether he was hearing cries of alarm or cries of pain. He kept his head down, expecting a return of fire.

It came, all right. All the rifles down below him were levelled at his rock and chips began to fly in all directions as he wriggled back, out of the danger zone. He was still pinned down by return fire when he started to hear sounds which suggested the opposition was getting to horse.

A loud voice said: 'Come on, boys, let's get out of here, the hombre over there in the rocks is done for in any case. And we have what we want, so let's go!'

Another man answered the call to action, and presently there were whinnying noises and general horse sounds. Hooves thundered on rock and small stones. The silence lengthened after the last fusillade of shooting. Sam risked looking out from his eyrie. He glanced first at the wrong spot. The ambushers had scrambled some fifty yards through the rocks in an easterly direction before getting to horse and riding forth.

Sam was slow to stand up. The quickness of the action had tired him. He raised his weapon to his shoulder, saw that the range was excessive, and changed his mind. He lowered the Winchester again, and instead, he glanced around in all directions, getting his whereabouts, and seeking the hiding place of the man on the opposite side.

A bay horse with its reins snagged over a low boulder suggested a direction. He called towards it, but received no reply. This did not deter him. He had to expect that the man he had fought for had possibly been hit by the curtain of lead sent against him.

Sam finger-combed his long hair. He then replaced his battered hat and started down to trail level. He had little fear of being under attack again now that the conspirators had left in a hurry. By the time he hit trail level, all that remained of them was a slight film of dust above the trail.

He called: 'Hey, you there! You in the rocks! Can you hear me?'

No human sound suggested that he had company. He whistled up the dun and waited for it, anxious to slake his thirst now that the action was over. The horse came willingly enough, but at a slow walk. As soon as it arrived, he took his canteen off the saddle and regaled himself with lukewarm water. The dun gave him a special look, one which could not be overlooked. He took the hint, pouring a small quantity of water into his hat for the animal to drink. They were both feeling a little better when they parted company again for the search to continue.

Sam began to walk up the centre of the track. His eyes were busy as he wandered along with his Winchester at the trail. Some two minutes had elapsed when he noticed where the rocks had been chipped by gunfire. He knew then that he was searching in the right area.

The crumpled body was not hard to find. He discovered it behind two projecting rocks, which were touching each other. The stricken man looked familiar. He had on a maroon vest, a grey stetson and trousers and a dark coat. His hair was black and his shirt front had been ruined by a seepage of blood from a wound caused by a ricochet.

Walter Lestrange had almost died before Sam had the time to interview him. He bent over the fallen man, ascertained by touching his eyelids that he still lived, and hurried away again in search of his canteen. He was breathless by the time he got back again.

The arrogant look was no longer on the man's face, but the eyes were clear, even though they mirrored pain. Sam propped him up and made him comfortable.

'Lestrange, I was ridin' after you to talk to you. Goodness knows how I managed to happen along jest at the time when you were bein' attacked by ambushers. Would you care to tell me anything about them?'

Lestrange shook his head. He did it in a gentle fashion, as though his neck was not particularly strong. 'So it's you, deputy. Well, I might have guessed you'd want to do some more talkin' before I was much older. You were fast off the mark, too, to have reached this place by this time. I don't have long. I guess you must think there is a connection between Pete Arnott an' myself. Well, I suppose you could say there is, but it ain't the one you probably have in mind. I'm not a member of any criminal organization, so you can put that right out of your head.'

Sam nodded. He would go along with Lestrange just so long as he received the sort of information he needed.

'So what is the connection, Lestrange?'

'I was actually on the premises of the hotel when the raid took place. I came across Pete prowling about down below, in and round the cellar where the wines are kept. Something about the way he acted made me want to help him.

'I took him up to ground level by another route and showed him a back door. I ushered him through the door and saw him make for the pinto horse which he had waiting for him out there. He made off, an' some time later I saw you prowlin' about in the alleyway.'

'I saw you bendin' over, close to the earth. It occurred to me then that you were studyin' the tracks made by the pinto. I saw you muster the posse some little time later and go off in pursuit. Anything else I claimed to know was jest sheer guesswork, havin' heard something of what you had done by Lesser Creek.'

Lestrange coughed. His life was obviously ebbing out of him, and yet he was not making any sort of an effort to call on Sam for any last consideration. Sam waited, and wondered. Was he looking down at a man who had master-minded a robbery, and then fallen out with his subordinates? Some-how, Walter Lestrange did not seem to fill the bill at this stage. Maybe he was just a bystander, after all, as he claimed.

'Why were you headin' for Great Wells in such a great hurry?' Sam asked him.

Lestrange managed a smile. 'I was leavin' Blackwood in a hurry, rather than seekin' to arrive in Great Wells. I think you'll learn more, after you've finished with me, but I want you to keep one thing always in mind. Pete Arnott might have turned renegade, but *I* never did. I was never a member of this gang, an' I couldn't tell you any details about my attackers, or about how they got onto me.'

'Why would they want to get onto you, at all?' Sam queried patiently.

The stricken man smiled with his eyes closed. 'Now that would be tellin',' he murmured in a faint voice. 'A man has to take one or two secrets with him to his death. Ain't that fair, amigo?'

Sam found himself nodding, as Lestrange's eyes opened wide, but he did not really know why he had agreed. The life ebbed out of the man he was holding almost at once. He lowered him to the ground, and walked away to collect the bay horse.

There was nothing special in the saddle pockets of the riderless horse to add anything to what Sam had already found out. He took the animal, with its saddle slackened, back to the place where its master had died. And there, screened from the corpse by a single well placed rock, he rolled himself a smoke and did nothing more until the burning part of it was close to his mouth. Having rubbed it out on his heel, he did some more thinking.

Here he was in between towns again, not many miles from the spot where Pete Arnott had died, and he had another corpse to deal with. This was getting to be a habit. Lestrange would have to be toted away from the spot, for the sake of everyone in Great Wells, or South Creek, who would be missing him.

Besides, there was that other fellow, the one he had shot off the top of the rock. He had probably died, too. What about him? He was about to go back and have a look for the body of the man who had fallen when another idea occurred to him.

While he was in the area, it would be as well to examine the rocks where the attackers had been hidden. It was just possible that he might find something else which would give him a lead in his current investigations.

Soon he was perched on the top of a low rock in front of the spot where the ambushers had crouched. The first thing he noticed, wedged against the foot of a huge boulder, was a leather bank money bag. He leapt down and examined it closely, and while he was busy he became aware of other things in the shape of fluttering pieces of paper.

The pieces of paper in fact were bank wrappers, the sort which are put round large wads of currency notes for easy handling. And the leather bag or satchel had the name of the Banker's Hotel bank printed on it.

He had stumbled upon evidence of the loot from the recent bank raid. One thing he did not know, and which he did not manage to work out for himself until some little time later, was that the loot had been slung over the saddle horn on Walter Lestrange's horse when he was first surprised by the ambushers.

The bag had bounced off his saddle before he went to earth in the rocks. His attackers had grabbed it. The decision to kill him before they moved on was another consideration. As Sam rose to his feet with the paper wrappers and the bank bag in his hand, however, he felt certain that he now knew the reason why the attackers had been attracted to Lestrange in such a vicious fashion.

In some way or another, the travelling wine salesman had managed to get his hands on the loot. And that was why he had left Blackwood in such a hurry.

8

Pangs of hunger were beginning to annoy Sam as he left the spot where he had found the money bag and made his way to the other place where his victim had fallen. The outlaw's body was not hard to find. He had fallen amid a small cluster of rocks, face downwards, but still alive.

The bullet lodged in the chest, along with injuries to vital parts caused by splintered ribs, had brought about the fellow's death. He had not moved more than a foot or two, since he dropped from above.

In appearance he was unprepossessing. He was in his early forties, bald across the crown with wispy black hair and bristling sideburns. His ears and brows showed more hair, of the tufted variety. His clothes were far from new, and not very clean.

He had died with his right index finger pointing to a small loose boulder about six inches away from his hand. Sam glanced towards it, and saw to his surprise that there was a sheet of paper underneath it. A message of some sort. He lifted the boulder and removed the outlaw's last earthly communication. It had been written with a blunt pencil, and addressed to 'The Finder.'

It said: *In exchange for a decent trail-side burial I'll give you one or two bits of information. If you are interested in locating other members of my renegade crew, keep watch on other Creek Basin towns, and look out for a man named Zeke Carver. Thanking you beforehand.*
　　　　　yours truly, Roscoe Lacey

Sam picked up the pencil, which was near to the left hand. He stuffed it in his shirt pocket as a souvenir, and reread Roscoe Lacey's letter. Obviously, the Creek Basin gang was going to be active in other towns of the basin, and a man named Zeke Carver was in some way involved.

He wondered who Carver was, and how he had incurred Lacey's displeasure. Carver had to be an enemy of Lacey's, even if he did not know it, otherwise the dying man would not have given away his name. But who was he? And what was his function with the outlaw gang?

Sam had a clue, but he wanted the solution to fall into his lap. This was unlikely to happen. After a brief pause, when he assessed the time of day as being after eight o'clock, he back-tracked to the two horses, and availed himself of a digging tool from the saddle of the bay. Of the outlaw's horse, there was no sign. Lacey's partners in crime must have taken it away with them.

In a space within a few yards of where the dead outlaw had fallen, Sam set to work with the spade. He spent over an hour digging the grave, and another half hour filling it in when Lacey was in place. After placing a wooden cross at the head and saying a couple of prayers which he had known all his life, he came away from the burial spot and returned to the place where Lestrange had chosen to defend himself.

Lestrange definitely had relations in the area; therefore, he would have to be taken into Great Wells the following morning.

The next thing was to build a fire and prepare a simple meal which could be taken as supper. This took a good half hour, and by the time the food was cooked and eaten, Sam was almost ready to turn in for the night. He availed himself of Lestrange's blanket and draped it over the corpse. Soon, he was curled up in his own blanket with only his head and shoulders showing, and with a cigarette protruding from his lips.

In the brightness of the blazing fire, he saw images. They intrigued him, as the warmth prepared him for the night.

For a time, he saw himself back along the reaches of the Lesser Creek with Pete Arnott. He recollected the time when they discovered a family of otters in the creek, and the fright they had had one time when a very youthful bear had strayed away from its mother and found their happy hunting grounds. Fortunately, they managed to stay well away from the mother bear when she came looking for her cub, but the size of her had given them both a shock and reminded them that not all animals were friendly to humans.

At one time, the two boys had swum the creek scores of times, trying to find out who could swim the greatest distance. There was little between them in that respect, but Sam was a superior swimmer when it came to under water work.

At fishing, they both excelled, and many a time they had taken home sufficient fish to feed both their families. On horseback, there was little to choose between them, but their attitude towards the quadrupeds was different. To Pete, they had just been a commodity of his father, or a beast to use for purposes of amusement. Sam saw them rather differently. He realized at an early age that the west would never have been opened up like it was, had it not been for the horse, man's chief servant.

When they were stripling youths, Mirabelle, who was five years younger than Pete, had merely been the little sister. For years she had no part in their games and goings on. It was only in the last four years that she had grown up sufficiently to take any special interest in what they did.

Around the time when the girl took on the form of a woman, there must have been a time when Arthur Arnott knew some disappointment in his son. Sam surmised that Arthur must always have wanted his son to take over the businesses which he had built up. It must have taken some little time for

Pete to establish in the mind of his parents that he had no special interest or aptitude for business. If Arthur had been disappointed over this, he had kept his strong feelings very much to himself.

Martha, Mrs Arnott, was an indulgent mother. She would have been the one to advise Arthur to sell out for the best money he could get, and thus have money in the bank for anything which the family might want to do.

Mirabelle was no idler. She had grown up able to help her mother in all departments of the home. She could prepare meals, wash, iron, do needlework, and supervise the work of others. In fact, the girl had had a very good grounding, where Pete's appeared to be sketchy.

The girl never needed any artificial aids for her appearance. Her long bell of auburn hair was a delight to behold, whether it was spilling out into the breeze from under a man's stetson, or tied sedately with a ribbon at the nape of her neck. Her body was long and shapely. She was a great favourite at the barn dances.

With a sigh, Sam came away from the past. Sooner or later, Arthur Arnott would have to tell his womenfolk how Sam was implicated in the death of Pete. However he said his piece, the two women, mother and daughter, were bound to have a great shock. The fact that someone they knew and trusted had actually pulled the trigger on the gun which killed Pete would materially alter their whole attitude towards Sam.

He would no longer be regarded as a friend of the family, nor could he ever hope to be a suitor for the hand of Mirabelle. In carrying out his duty in the way in which he thought was justified, he had spoiled his own prospects with the family. Even his job might have to be sacrificed, if Arnott had his way, and that might mean a complete change of life.

The more he thought over the situation, the more Sam felt that he would go to any lengths to avoid meeting Mirabelle. After all, she had applauded his fighting with Lestrange, after the latter had hinted that he — Sam — had shot Pete. Whatever would the girl think when she found that Lestrange had only aired the truth, and that Sam was her brother's killer?

And now Lestrange had bowed out, due to an outlaw's bullet. Yet another young man closely involved in Sam's life was ready for an early grave. He had it in him to hope that no one thought he had been the one to shoot Lestrange. The weight of his guilt in regard to Pete was as much as Sam could bear.

At long last, he began to feel really sleepy. Among his last remembered thoughts, he wondered if it would be easier to talk with the Lestrange family about their loss than it was to talk to the Arnotts. And then he fell asleep.

★ ★ ★

The big black-handed clock on the wall of the mortician's shop in Great Wells was almost exactly pointing to ten o'clock when Sam reined in under it and dismounted. He had with him Walter Lestrange's body draped over the steaming bay horse which had belonged to the deceased man.

The undertaker appeared in the shop doorway as though he had been waiting for Sam. He was a tall bulky individual of about sixty years, with puffed out cheeks, a drooping white moustache and clip-on spectacles. He straightened out the brim of an expensive black stetson and thrust out his hand in Sam's direction.

'Glad to meet you, deputy. I'm Harman Grice, the undertaker in these parts. I see you've brought me some business there. Would you care to give me a few details?'

Sam nodded and drew the fellow indoors. Nearly a dozen townsfolk were clustering around the tired bay and wondering if they knew the man

120

jack-knifed across its back.

Sam said, indoors: 'I'm Sam Regan, operatin' out of the sheriff's office.' He pulled off his white bandanna, and dabbed himself with it. 'The dead man is known as Walter Lestrange. As far as I can tell his folks live in South Creek. He's a wine saleman, I believe. Yesterday, he was shot on the trail north of here by a bunch of renegades, who took away from him something they thought to be very valuable. I think that's about all the details you need to know, for now, Mr Grice. Lestrange was booked in at the Holborn Hotel. I guess I'll mosey along there an' tell the manager he won't be arrivin'. See you later, amigo.'

Grice, who was a jovial fellow, in spite of his rather dismal profession, intimated that he had met the widow Lestrange in the town when she came in shopping. He also said that he would have Walter's body brought indoors and measured up, prior to other arrangements being made.

Sam left him, asked a bystander to take his horse to the livery, and walked along to the Holborn Hotel which was in the east end of town.

James Smith, the hotel manager, was just having a confidential chat with his male receptionist, prior to going out for refreshment to a coffee bar. He was a burly, bronzed ex-prize-fighter from Manchester, England, with a slightly flattened nose. He had on a smart brown suit and a derby hat.

Sam perceived by the deference shown to Smith, that he was, indeed, the Boss of the place. He butted in, showed his badge and gave his name. When the introductions were completed, he buttonholed the manager and drew him aside.

'Mr Smith, one of your clients who booked in from the county seat will not be turning up. As a matter of fact, I've jest had to deliver him to Harman Grice's establishment. There is a small way in which you could help me. I have to trace the family of this man who has died. Name of Lestrange. Would you be good enough to check if there is any mail waitin' for him?'

Smith wanted to help. He rounded the counter himself and found the letter addressed to Walter Lestrange Esq, in the pigeon hole with the letter 'L' on it. In full view of Smith, Sam opened the letter, glanced briefly at its contents, and read out from it the address of the writer.

'This has come from a Mrs Catherine Lestrange, of Creek View Villa, South Creek. I shall have to get in touch with her personally. It isn't the thing to send messages about deaths over the wire. So I'll retain the letter for the time being, Mr Smith, an' take myself along to the town marshal's office, to put him in the picture.'

Smith walked along with Sam as far as the town marshal's office and on the way, he confirmed that he had known Walter Lestrange, and that the deceased had been in the habit of calling at his hotel and checking the contents of the wine cellar from time to time.

Smith was no great friend of Lestrange's. The latter just came and went every few weeks, and that was all. He stayed in a room at the hotel on all his visits.

Veteran Marshal Herb Tyson was delighted to see Sam, and also keen to hear all the details of the Creek Basin gang's recent ambush out of town. The interview lasted some thirty minutes. As soon as it was over, the wires began to hum as the information was broadcasted by telegraph.

Sam did not stay in town long. He started out for South Creek on the back of a borrowed grey stallion.

9

Harman Grice, the mortician, was the man to make the grey stallion available to Sam. It was one of a string of three which the undertaker kept as his sole sign of affluence. The animal was low in the barrel, and it did not have the dun quarter horse's fast turn of speed, but it did have plenty of stamina, and that was what counted in a headlong dash from one town to another when the time was dictated by a corpse and the wishes of the bereaved. The time was around eleven o'clock when the hurrying sheriff's deputy left the outskirts of Great Wells and started upon the journey to South Creek. The latter town was one of the smallest and most isolated of the Creek Basin towns and it was one in which Sam had not really spent a lot of time.

Marshal Herb Tyson, of Great Wells,

knew the town better. He was also something of an expert on the local geography which meant that he was in a position to advise Sam upon his journey to the southernmost outpost of the basin.

South Creek was ten miles east-south-east of Great Wells, along a trail which gradually went further away from the principal waterway, so that South Creek itself was as far as five miles removed from the Little Pecos.

Sam had done a lot of riding of late, and yet he was not sorry to have done so. In fact, the riding blended in with his general restlessness and his out-of-sorts feeling which had beset him ever since the clash with Pete.

He found the trail was a hard one upon horses. Very soon the straining grey was blowing hard. He allowed it to rest at the top of the many gradients, but he did not permit any lengthy rests. He figured that the animal could rest after the trip to South Creek was over; always, he was conscious of the passing of time.

In a way, he began to think it might have been better to send the sad news of Lestrange's death through by telegraph, and address it to the town marshal, or some senior townsman, who could have been made responsible to break the news.

After all, it was going to shake the mother, and she would have to think very seriously about a place of interment without delay. In that part of the world, it was not considered a good thing to delay a burial. Weighing it up all over again, Sam found himself shrugging.

He had his sense of decent behaviour mixed up with his duty once again. He wanted the Lestrange woman to have what comfort she could glean from a sympathetic personal messenger who had been the last to see her son alive, and he also wanted to talk to her in his official capacity as sheriff's deputy looking into the matter of the bank robbery and the subsequent events.

As the deceased was nearly thirty, Sam assumed that the woman he was going to see would be at least fifty years of age. A woman of mature years, perhaps a little like Martha Arnott, except that she was widowed. One of his contacts had described her as a widow. He wondered how long she had been without her husband, and whether his death had soured her.

Such contemplations helped him to sit out the miles on the saddle which was better adjusted to the contours of another horse's back.

* * *

Around noon that day, Catherine Lestrange was in the back room of a ladies' hat and gown shop at the fashionable end of South Creek's Main Street. In a recess away from the packing cases and other articles, she was taking coffee on the visitor's side of a broad desk belonging to a Miss Effie Ellingham, the owner of the establishment.

Miss Ellingham was a tall thin blonde woman of fifty, a contemporary of Catherine Lestrange, who was, in fact, two years her junior.

Mrs Lestrange was a tall dark brunette, with jet black hair which still had the same quality in it as when she had been a young and eligible woman. At that particular time, although it was long, she had it pinned up on the top of her head under a small becoming black bonnet.

Middle age had added a few pounds to the widow's nicely rounded frame, and she had used her curves well assisted by a good tailor. Effie Ellingham was a milliner and a tailor, and her attentions to Kate Lestrange had resulted in their growing friendship over a number of years.

On the desk between them were two expensive items. One was a fur stole with expensive metal fastenings, and the other was a wide-brimmed pink bonnet with a reddish veil of some flimsy material.

Effie Ellingham remarked: 'Really, Kate, I don't know how you manage to keep all those rich suitors at bay, dressing the way you do, and with your looks. In fact, as your friend, I'm surprised you don't hook one of them without any further delay. After all, that house, Creek View Villa, must be an expensive one to run, an' if you had a rich husband you could more or less please yourself how much you spent on clothes and other adornments, dear.'

The visitor nodded and smiled indulgently. She dabbed away from her skirt an imaginary drop of coffee with a small square lace handkerchief. Then she smoothed down the lush green velvet.

'I know, I know, dear Effie. When the men come around I'm always tempted, especially when I think of my expensive tastes, and the cost of living. But in holding them at bay, I suppose I'm considering Walter, really. He's such a fine boy, and he often says he's stayed a bachelor so as not to have a woman come between him and me.

'It's so nice to have a boy think so much of his mother, don't you think?'

The proprietress traced the line of her finely arched brows and nodded very decidedly. She glanced down at the two items on the desk, both of which her customer had tried on and found to her liking.

'So you'd like me to put these two things on one side for a little while, Kate? I don't suppose any of the other women in this town would have shown any interest in them, anyway. Yes, I'll keep them here in the back room until you tell me what you want done with them.'

Kate Lestrange leaned forward and squeezed the other woman's ringed hand. 'If you would be so kind as to hold them for me, jest for a short time, dear Effie. As a matter of fact, I'm dying for Walter to get back to town. He sent me a wire the other day which suggested in a roundabout sort of way that we might be in substantial funds in the near future. So I'm hopin' that his plans will have matured quite soon.'

Miss Ellingham chuckled into her handkerchief. 'If Walter is in funds, then I shan't be keepin' the stole and the hat for very long. I wonder what you would think if he came home with a rich bride? How would you feel about that, Kate?

Mrs Lestrange's rich Cupid's bow mouth opened in sudden surprise. She frowned with annoyance, and only recovered her poise with an effort.

'Dear Effie, you shocked me! Tell me you don't think it's really a possibility, that you were only joking!'

The door bell at the front of the establishment indicated the arrival of a new customer. Miss Ellingham at once rose to her feet, indicating that Kate might stay where she was, but the latter was ready to move on. She detained her friend long enough to be assured that her last suggestion had, indeed, only been a joke thought up on the spur of the moment, and then walked after her into the other part of the shop through the bead curtain.

Mrs Lestrange took her leave rather formally. This was for the benefit of a rather portly woman accompanied by her husband, a hatchet-faced individual in a derby hat and a brown checked suit. Five minutes later, the widow was seated at her usual table in the nearby restaurant.

Creek View Villa was one of a pair of white-painted two-storey semi-detached houses on a short street built on high ground.

Sam Regan walked the borrowed grey stallion up to the rail just outside the narrow front garden and tied it up there a little after two o'clock in the afternoon. He had slackened the saddle and rocked it by the time the owner of the house next door became aware of his presence.

The observer was a retired something or other connected with a railroad. He did a little gardening in the afternoons in his shirt sleeves and a straw hat. He was a fat, stooping sixty year old who looked to be about seventy.

'Son, even I with my short sight can tell you are fresh off the trail. If you are thinkin' of payin' court to the comely Mrs Lestrange you'd best slip round the back before she gets home and duck your head underneath the pump! Give that hoss of yours a treat, too. You'll find a bucket.'

Sam nodded, grinned and hesitated.

'Go on, go right ahead. Kate might not be all that flush with cash these days but she never would refuse a ridin' man the use of her pump. So make the best of the opportunity, 'cause if you don't, she's goin' to take one look at you an' ask you to come back in the evenin' when the goin' ain't so hot. Take the advice of an old man who knows the widow!'

The neighbour was filling his lungs to expand on his knowledge of the widow, but Sam waved him into silence and at once stepped through the small gate and made his way around the side of the house to the rear. He found the pump, as the old man had explained, and made good use of the bucket. After tossing the first gallon of water over his own head and neck, he refilled the bucket and took it around for the horse. He allowed it to drink a few pints, and then withdrew the bucket, wiping it down with a few handfuls of grass to help it cool down.

By the time the widow came up the street under her pale green sun parasol, Sam had freshened up quite considerably and was sitting on the three steps at the front of the house. She saw the stallion before she saw its owner, and her eyes, hidden by the parasol's brim, showed pleased surprise that her visitor was a man from out of town.

A womanly caprice made her act in an offhand manner with him, as though she wanted to have him off the premises with the least possible delay. The neighbour stayed around just long enough to see the reception she gave to Sam, and then he went off round the back, grinning to himself and shaking his head.

Sam stood up, hat in hand. 'Mrs Catherine Lestrange, ma'am?'

'Yes, I'm Kate Lestrange, but I'm tellin' you at the outset, Mr Deputy, that I don't feel much feel in the mood for talking with peace officers on a hot afternoon.'

Sam nodded rather formally and stepped away from the place where he had been seated. 'I can quite understand that, ma'am, but I bring the kind of news which can't be put off. It is my wish that I shouldn't have to be the bearer of bad news, but I have news for you, and it isn't good. It concerns Walter Lestrange, who, I believe, is your son.'

Mention of bad news and Walter had the immediate effect of killing Catherine's play-acting. She murmured: 'Walter is in some kind of trouble?'

'He *was* in trouble, only yesterday, on the other side of Great Wells. Mrs Lestrange, I can't keep you in suspense.

I'm afraid Walter isn't ever coming back home. You see, he's dead.'

Catherine caught hold of an upright supporting the porch. Sam moved towards her, but she did not require his supporting hand. She moved up the steps and indicated that she wanted him to follow her indoors. Sam was ushered into the lounge, which was a small but tastefully furnished room at the front of the house.

Mrs Lestrange went through to the kitchen and put a kettle on the stove. When she came back, her face was pale but resolute. She had taken off her hat and was prepared to sit and talk about the whys and wherefores of Walter's death.

'Where is he now?'

'He's at the undertakers at Great Wells. As a matter of fact, Mr Grice is standing by to await your instructions. All you have to do is get in touch by telegraph. Incedentally, the death occurred yesterday evening.'

'Was it — accidental?'

'No, I'm afraid it wasn't. There was a shootin' incident on the trail. The way things turned out, Walter was ambushed by outlaws. He had something which they dearly wanted to lay their hands on. After they had it, they took his life. He fought, but they outnumbered him. I happened along a short while too late to save him. He was still alive when I got to him, but he couldn't tell me anything about the men who attacked him. It's all very sad, an' I wish it was different, but jest wishin' don't alter things. If you could bear up for a little while, I'd like to ask you one or two questions. After that, I'll help in any way I can. I was the one who brought his body into Great Wells, but I guess you will have realized that.'

Catherine's mouth was set in a hard line when she went to the kitchen to brew the coffee. When she came back again with it, however, she was perfectly composed. She served for them both and then sat back, awaiting questions.

'I gather from enquiries I've been

makin' that Walter had something to do with supplyin' Holborn hotels with wine. Can you tell me anything about that, Mrs Lestrange?'

'Certainly. My maiden name was Catherine Holborn. I'm the daughter of Charles Holborn, the one who started the famous chain of Holborn hotels. Since my father died, the bulk of the income from the hotels and the actual estate has gone to my brother, Victor, who has settled on the east coast. I was left a thousand dollars or so, but that has been swallowed up, you might say by widowhood.

'I shall be poorer, now that Walter is dead. But I guess I can put up with it. If the prospect is too lowering, I can marry some rich suitor, or another. But you were asking about Walter. As the grandson of the Holborn founder, he was left the right to inspect the wine cellars and to supply wines when they were needed. He made a small income from it. There was never a lot of money in it.

'And now I should like to ask a question. Why was he killed? What was it he had that outlaws wanted to get their hands on?'

'Money, Mrs Lestrange. A good deal of money. I think he must have found it in the wine cellar of the Bankers' Hotel in Blackwood. But it wasn't honest money. It was that stolen from the bank in the recent raid. Somebody must have had the idea of hiding it all, or some of it, in the cellars underneath the hotel.'

At that point, Catherine Lestrange's poise let her down. She dabbed her eyes with a handkerchief and rocked herself in the chair.

To comfort her, Sam said: 'Before he died, Walter assured me he had no dealings with the outlaws, and if it is any consolation to you, I believed him. It's a great pity, the way things have turned out. May I ask if you want the burial to take place here, or in Great Wells?'

The speed with which the bereaved

woman gave her decision surprised Sam.

'I think I'd like to have him buried in Great Wells. Don't ask me why. It's jest a feeling I have. Will you help me with the arrangements?'

'Of course.'

Sam pulled his chair a little closer and gazed earnestly into her face.

10

Before four o'clock that same afternoon, Sam was on the way back to Great Wells. He had talked and discussed the situation of Walter Lestrange's death with the widowed mother, and had come away with certain specific instructions for the burial, and for informing one or two notable families in the Creek Basin.

As he rode the sweating grey, his mind went back over the interview with the widow. She had proved an interesting woman, and a strong one, judging by the way in which she had borne up under the distressing news.

Her interest in what he had said had seemed to deepen when he mentioned the wine cellars under the Bankers' Hotel. A lot of young Lestrange's business seemed to take place in the lower regions of the hotels, and Sam found himself wondering if there was anything of a secret nature behind Walter's study of the cellars.

His grandfather, Charles Holborn, had been a great eccentric. Was it beyond the bounds of possibility that he might have left something special in the basements of his hotels for his grandson to find? If Catherine Lestrange and her son, Walter, had been left barely provided for, was it not possible that something might have been hidden in one or more of the cellars? Some secret bonus in the form of money, which the grandson could collect for himself, provided he did his job of inspecting in a thoroughly businesslike way.

In Sam's estimation, such a procedure was a foolish way to go about things. For instance, any casual worker at the hotels whose business it was to bring up a few bottles of wine might chance upon the hidden treasure, whatever it was. Wine waiters, and similarly employed people, often sought the opportunity to go down the cellars and have a secret glass of wine, or to take a smoke when they ought to have been busy at their work between rooms and the bars.

Even if there was little in this rather outlandish theory, Walter Lestrange had been down below when Pete Arnott, well away from the parts of the hotel used by ordinary patrons, bumped into him on his way up. Walter had seen Pete off the premises, and, being something of an expert on the lower regions of the hotel, he had made his discovery some time later.

It would be interesting to know whether Pete had taken the loot down below with the full knowledge and backing of the other renegades, or whether it had been his own idea to take the loot below. Perhaps he had been hiding it without anyone else knowing, but that did not seem likely. Some of the loot must have surely been taken out by the front door.

If Pete had been acting on his own, he must have wanted to keep in touch with the other outlaws, otherwise he would not have ridden after them in order to rejoin them.

By seven in the evening, the somewhat tired young man had arrived at his destination. He took coffee with Herb Tyson, the veteran marshal, ate a meal in the Holborn Hotel, along with manager James Smith and undertaker Harman Grice. Gradually, he made over the requests of Mrs Lestrange concerning the burial and the reception, which was to take place at the hotel.

An hour later, he left his associates for the town's telegraph office where he sent off no less than four telegraph messages. One of them gave him little cause for ease of mind. Catherine was sending for Arthur Arnott from the county seat. Catherine, Sam recollected, had not been among the mourners for Pete Arnott, but nevertheless she was summoning to Great Wells for the burial the man whom Sam least wanted to see.

★ ★ ★

At the burial, on the following afternoon, Sam stayed well back in the
crowd, sided by Marshal Tyson and
James Smith. He had seen the Arnotts
arrive, all three, and the sight of them
had filled him with foreboding. One
glance from the women showed that
they had learned the awful secret about
Pete's killer. Sam was so distressed that
he wondered if they would expect him
to seek them out and make contact, or
whether they would expect him to keep
well out of the way.

As the service came to an end, and
the mourners streamed back towards
the main thoroughfare, Herb Tyson and
James Smith stayed close to the fair
young deputy, who was wearing a black
bandanna for the occasion. They sided
him all the way back to the hotel and
sat beside him at the table for the eating
of the meal.

When the feeding was about over,
Smith led the way into the bar and

himself poured drinks for the marshal and the deputy sheriff. Over their whisky, they chatted quietly, watching the comings and goings from the dining room, and quietly admiring the beauty and dignity of the chief mourner.

A scrubbed callused hand descended upon the fair young man's shoulder, heralding a meeting he had been dreading. With false warmth, Arthur Arnott called: 'Well, howdy, young Sam, it ain't often the likes of you an' me bump into each other outside of the county seat. I wonder if you could spare me a few minutes of your valuable time? That is, if these gents don't mind me hornin' in?'

Smith and the marshal both turned warmly towards the retired liveryman and made it clear that they had no prior claims upon Sam's time. They knew Arnott reasonably well, on account of his having set up house near to the town.

Arnott pushed and jostled his way out of the bar without undue haste.

He talked here and there to his aquaintances and said a few appropriate things about how the funeral service had gone.

The Arnott buckboard was one of several outside, waiting for the owners to emerge.

I'm thinking of takin' this vehicle into the livery, but first I thought you might ride a little way with me, to kind of bring me up to date, Sam.'

'If that's the way you want things, then I'll be glad to go along with you, Mr Arnott. I can't think that this interview is likely to be a pleasant one, though, especially as it follows right after a funeral.'

Sam climbed up on the seat; Arnott did the same and took the reins. Soon they were jogging up the street, weaving to get through other parked traffic and walked horses.

Arthur remarked: 'Yes, it sure is strange to have you attendin' another funeral so soon. Another of the country's eligible young bachelors again. And you the last man to see the deceased alive again. It's gettin' to be a habit with you. You must be gettin' used to it. Tell me, how exactly did Walter Lestrange meet his death?'

'You've heard on the details in town, Mr Arnott,' Sam pointed out.

'Jest the same I'd like to hear them from your own lips, Sam. I figure it won't do you a deal of harm to repeat them once again.'

Sam glared briefly at his interrogator, but he said nothing to fan the other's anger. 'Lestrange was caught and jumped by outlaws along the turn-off towards East Halt. The thing they were after, the money bag, must have bounced off his saddle while the pursuit was still on.

'They grabbed it and took it into the rocks with them. Some men would have merely emptied a few rounds of ammunition into the rocks around their enemy, but this crowd were keen to see him dead. They were still shootin' at him when I got there, although they had wounded him already in such a way that he was dying.'

Arnott flicked the reins as they left town, and shot Sam a sidelong glance. 'You say Walter had this money, outlaw money you called it to others. And that they attacked him to get it back again. Where did Walter get it from? The folks here in Great Wells seem to think Lestrange had merely found it.'

'That's a good question, Mr Arnott. Walter found it in the basement of the Bankers' Hotel, in the spot where your son, Pete, had hidden it. It was part of Walter's business in life to examine the hotel wine cellars. He was down there on the day of the raid, and that made him bump into Pete as Pete was tryin' to find his way up again.'

Arnott gave an angry chuckle. 'Now, hold on a minute, young man, take it easy. You'll have to prove it to me to have me believe that Pete was down there doin' anything at all with outlaw money. So talk, and make it sound good. You have a lot at stake.'

Sam was surprised at his own calmness, in the face of provocation. He had expected his word to be challenged and in no uncertain fashion, but Arnott was certainly making no secret of his great hostility. The deputy fished in his shirt pocket and brought out the pieces of paper which had been found beside the trail around the time of Lestrange's death.

'You see these, Mr Arnott? They were ripped off large wads of currency notes when the outlaws recovered the money from the bag which Walter Lestrange was carrying. I don't have the bag now. I left it in town.

'I talked to Lestrange before he died. His exact words were, 'Pete Arnott might have turned renegade but I never did.' And that was the testimony of a dying man. He also explained how he had found Pete wandering about in the basement of the hotel, how he had shown him a staircase which led towards the alley at the side.

'He saw Pete mount up on the pinto

horse and ride after the other renegades. He also saw me arrive a little
while later and discover the tracks of
the pinto, an' the shoe which made a
definite pattern which could be followed. He was actually guessing when
he sent a message to you about my
havin' killed Pete. Does that meet with
your approval?'

'How could it do that?' Arnott
returned bitterly. 'How could a man
approve of details connected with his
son's death, and under a cloud, into the
bargain? You're tellin' me that you have
found enough to satisfy yourself that
Pete was definitely in cahoots with bad
men, an' I can tell you that I don't like
it!'

By this time, the vehicle was a good
half mile clear of town. Arnott braked
hard and turned it, pulling viciously
upon the reins as he did so. As he
worked, so Sam's temper flared.

'Well, if you don't like it you'll have
to go to blazes, Arthur Arnott. You've
masqueraded as a big shot for as long

as I can remember. How does it feel to know that you are the father of a renegade, a man who but for the kindness of friends would be branded as an outlaw throughout the whole country! I don't have to fear you! If I do, it'll mean that law and order an' ordinary everyday justice don't function any more!

'How would you like it if I spread it around the Basin towns how Pete Arnott dallied with me, fired four shots at me, in an attempt to kill me, and how he helped to rob the Bankers' Hotel? Do you think your womenfolk could stand up to the harshness of public opinion?

'Most men would believe me if I made it known, because one thing I've done while I've been in office. I've established a reputation for honesty, and even you can't take that away from me! Now, I've finished talkin' so say anythin' you've got to say. Only remember this, when we get back I ain't harin' around the county jest to get information for your biassed ears! I'm doin' it to confound a gang bent on more damage, more robberies. Hear me?'

Sam was sufficiently heated to have gone on for some time, but somehow he dried up and that was the end of his talk.

As they entered the streets again, Arnott murmured: 'If you ever do spread it around about Pete, so that my womenfolk suffer, you'll have another Arnott after your blood, an' this one has had a bit more experience in the use of firearms.'

Sam shrugged. He maintained a strict silence until they were outside of the hotel once more. There, by coincidence, Mirabelle and her mother had just emerged. The women waved, checked their obvious pleasure at seeing Arthur and solemnly nodded and smiled to Sam. He doffed his hat and returned the smile, while Arthur left the buckboard and stamped off into the hotel bar without exchanging a word with anyone.

'Here's your chance for a slight change of atmosphere, Mirabelle,' Sam called, acting impulsively. 'Get aboard and take a run up the street before the horses get too tired of comin' and going.'

She murmured: 'I'm not at all sure that this sort of merriment is the thing after attendin' a funeral, Sam. After all, Mrs Lestrange might appear again an' she might think badly of us.'

'From what I learned yesterday, Mirabelle, Mrs Lestrange is a broad-minded woman. She does not go lookin' for trouble behind the known facts. I'm sure she would wish us well if she saw us at this moment.'

Sam coaxed a better speed out of the horses than their owner had done. He saw this as an opportunity to make sure that the girl knew the truth, whatever her father said when they were alone together. He admitted to having killed Pete, and having kept the matter a secret for the sake of the family as well as for himself. He told all the details which he had found out, and he concluded by adding a little of something else which had occurred to him as he was talking.

'I don't know why I'm thinkin' so jest at this juncture, but it's jest possible there might be some sort of a hidden link-up between the Holborn hotels and the doings of the Creek Basin gang. I wouldn't be at all surprised if the Holborn chain of hotels was involved in some strike of the future.'

The buckboard was half way back again before Mirabelle ventured to make known the state of her mind.

'Sam, my father is a dominatin' character. I have to go along with a lot that he says. I don't like myself for sayin' this, but I believe all that you've told me about — about Pete and Walter Lestrange. I don't *want* to believe, but I can't help myself. Somehow or another we've all failed Pete, otherwise he wouldn't take up with outlaws and excuse himself on the grounds of boredom.

'I want you to stay away from us Arnotts for a while, till we've grown used to the new state of affairs. But if you do stay away, don't go thinkin' that we're all your enemies. I think you must suffer enough, privately, havin' been the one to pull the trigger. So rest assured, I'll be feelin' for you.'

With his emotions freshly churned up inside him, Sam thanked her and left her outside the hotel. He was glad that Arthur was not out looking for them.

11

On account of the fact that she was a relation of the founder, Catherine Lestrange was given a small private sitting room for the day in a part of the Holborn Hotel in Great Wells. Around nine o'clock in the evening, Sam went along to Mrs Lestrange, knowing that she would very likely leave town at an early hour the following morning.

She waved him into a seat, and the only sign of stress which she showed was when she blew her nose hard in a pocket handkerchief.

'Well then, Sam, there must have been something else of passin' importance you wanted to say to me before the day of the burial is over. What was it you wanted to discuss?'

'Mrs Lestrange, I hardly know where to begin. Perhaps I should jest say that I have a theory that there is a connection between the outlaw raiders and the Holborn hotels.'

Clapping her hands to the sides of her head, Catherine showed signs of great surprise. 'You surely can't be meaning that the Holborn hotels are run by a criminal organization! Tell me it isn't that, Sam! I couldn't bear it after what's happened, even though they might as well have been started by a complete stranger for what benefit I'm gettin' from them now.'

'I mean that somebody in some way connected with the hotels might be in cahoots with the outlaws, that's all. Maybe you could help me. I don't think we'll be lookin' for somebody who has worked for the combine for a long time. It might be somebody who's happened along in the past few months. For a start, do you know anybody by the name of Zeke, or Ezekiel Carver?'

Catherine swayed in a kind of a shrug and shook her head. 'That name doesn't mean anything to me. Is there any special reason why it should?'

'Not really. It was jest a chance. A dying outlaw told me to look out for a man of that name, it's part of my investigation, you see. I know for a fact there's no one at this hotel with a name like that, because I've already looked. And you'll know the names of men who work in the hotel on South Creek, I suppose.'

The widow nodded. 'Mark Durbin, the manager in my town, has been around for quite a while, but I can tell you of one newcomer. He's the manager of the hotel in East Halt. I did hear his name mentioned, but I've forgotten it now. If you're lookin' for a newcomer he might be your man, but I wouldn't like to say. I don't have any special knowledge of the man, or of anyone with criminal intent, for that matter.'

Sam leaned forward, toying with his hat brim. 'Mrs Lestrange, it occurs to me that Walter perhaps never visited the new man in East Halt. Would you mind a great deal if I went along to that town

160

and represented myself as your son? I know it's askin' a lot, but it might get me into the place without a lot of fuss. Nobody came from East Halt to the funeral, did they?'

'No, they didn't. It does seem a little strange to masquerade as the dead, but if you think it will help you to get closer to the men who shot Walter, then by all means go ahead. I have a valise full of his clothes with me right here. Maybe you could wear one of his suits, if you really wanted to look like him. I'm sure I don't mind, if you don't.'

Sam jumped at the idea of thus changing his appearance. He left the widow's sitting room carrying the valise, and in his temporary room he tried on one of Walter's outfits. The grey stetson was a little tight across the brow and had to be worn further back than usual. The black coat was also tight, across his shoulders; but by wearing it unbuttoned, it was possible to get around that difficulty as well.

★ ★ ★

When Sam left Great Wells the following day he was wearing his own clothes. The transformation into the guise of Walter Lestrange took place about two miles out from East Halt at half past eleven in the morning. He was riding his own dun horse. He figured that if the manager of the hotel did not know Walter Lestrange, then he would also lack knowledge of the type of horse the salesman rode.

Wilbur West, the new manager of the hotel, was sitting in his office with a pair of unaccustomed spectacles hooked across his nose. He took them off rather hastily when Sam knocked and entered, and massaged the mark they had made on the bridge of his nose.

West was a man in his early forties; he wore a brown jacket and riding breeches and black gaiters. He had a limp dating from the days when he had been much more active on horseback.

He was of medium height, with a long Syrian nose and a lantern jaw which made him look a very positive character. His black hair was receding a little at the temples. He studied Sam with an exceptionally sharp pair of eyes.

'Good day to you, mister. What can I do for you? Are you lookin' for accommodation?'

Sam studied the name board in the front of the desk. He replied: 'Howdy, Mr West. No, I'm not lookin' for accommodation. I call here regularly to deal with the matter of wines. I have this concession from the Holborn management. I'm related through my mother to the founder.'

Sam showed one of the business cards which had been in Lestrange's valise. West was suitably impressed when he saw the printed pasteboard. He asked again, wondering how best to handle this man who had the confidence of the general management.

'If you could give me a list of the wines you have in stock, I'd be obliged.

163

And list of the names of members of staff who have the handling of them. Then I can go away and study the list. I'll come back to check the cellars later in the day. Perhaps this afternoon, if that meets with your approval?'

As a newcomer West had wanted to show his efficiency. He produced a wine stock list from a drawer, and a list of the names of all staff from a sheaf of papers hanging on a wall hook.

'All right, Mr Lestrange. Here are the facts you want. Stick around. Make use of the hotel for any of your needs. You'll find me in and around the building throughout all the day, in one spot or another. Ask the receptionist for the key to the room you generally use. We must make sure you are properly dealt with, an' that's for sure. It ain't every day a man meets a direct descendant of Charles Holborn, no siree.'

After replying suitably, Sam left the room. At the reception desk, he found that the clerk had gone on an errand. He knew, however, from a diary found among Lestrange's possessions, which room he usually occupied. The key was on the rack, and he took it.

In the privacy of the small room, he checked through the list of employees. None of them in name looked anything like Zeke Carver. He was disappointed. Later, he checked through the admission register, and there again he drew a blank. Of the elusive Carver, there was no sign; he was nowhere about, unless he was masquerading under another name.

★　★　★

Sam took his meal at an eating house near the other end of the town, so as to widen his acquaintance with the local people. When he had finished he asked the Asiatic proprietor if he had come across a man by the name of Carver.

The Chinese knew the names of few white acquaintances and he had little conversation, either. Sam visited a barber for a haircut and a shave, and the barber, a Mexican, also claimed not to know anyone of that name. After visiting three bars and getting no further at all in his search for the elusive renegade, he began to take life easier.

What, after all, was there to suggest that Carver would be in East Halt? He, Sam, was in East Halt for two reasons. One, because the manager of the Holborn Hotel in the town was a newcomer. And two, because the outlaws who had killed Walter Lestrange had travelled in the direction of East Halt, after recovering the bank money.

Basin County was a big area. The man with the unusual name might be almost anywhere. Or he might have moved out of the area altogether, looking for somewhere else to perpetrate his evil deeds — if indeed he was a criminal. There was nothing at all to support the dead outlaw's claim that Carver was an outlaw. It might have been a name conjured out of the dying man's imagination.

Sam sighed. Having reasoned his hopes to their lowest ebb, he then retraced his steps to the Holborn Hotel and made his way inside. The elderly female receptionist was yawning behind the desk by that time. Sam wondered whether to by-pass her, and decided not to. Instead, he stepped up to the counter and asked the way down to the wine cellar.

'I talked with Mr West this morning and he suggested that it would be in order for me to make a routine check of the wine cellars this afternoon. Perhaps you would be kind enough to show me the way down below.'

The woman approved of his appearance. She nodded, lit a lamp which was hanging above the counter, and preceded Sam down a back corridor which had doors opening off it. She selected one on the right, and it opened under pressure with a slight squeak.

'Here you are then, Mr Lestrange. You'll want the lamp with you. Mr West said for me to look out for you. Mind how you go. The steps are a little worn. I'll be behind the counter if there's anything else you want.'

Sam smiled and thanked her. He went down the steps with great care and pulled up at the bottom, confronted by a cellar full of wine racks and barrels. To one side there was a brick or stone archway leading through into another cellar. Down below, the hotel was quite extensive.

There were many cobwebs about, and the state of the double cellar suggested that no one spent any time in cleaning it. He surmised that it only had an occasional visit from a wine waiter, when certain stocks on the floor above had to be replenished.

He had no intention of checking the whole stock of wines, but this was an opportunity to examine in detail the possible hiding places for anything of value, which an eccentric founder might leave behind for a descendant in charge of the wines.

As far as hiding anything went, there were few permanent places which a careful man might use. Bricked in windows served as shelves and there was a small lift connected with the floor above which had not been used to send up wine for many a long year. The rope which held up the lift had been severed at some point and the wine lift would not leave the basement level without being pushed.

Holding the lamp a little way above his head, Sam studied the walls. He was half way along one of the walls through the archway when the smallest of sounds not made by himself made him stiffen. He was just in the act of turning his head when a blunt instrument of some weight connected with the back of his head.

The blow fell with sickening force, and he slid to the ground and toppled over. The hand which had struck the blow caught the lamp and dexterously whipped it away before it could be smashed.

With all the power of his will, Sam fought off the lassitude which was the forerunner of unconsciousness. The man who had bent over him was just visible in an odd detail or two where the lamp shed its light. A grey bandanna mask was draped across the lower part of the face. The hair was thick, short and curly, being blue-black in colour on the head and in the eyebrows. Eyes almost as dark as the hair radiated flashing glances in Sam's direction.

The man was talking, slowly and softly, as though he did not want to be overheard. Sam's senses swam. The man's profile began to come and go. As the outline of the man undulated, Sam's consciousness slowly ebbed away. And yet he heard a little more of what the man was saying before he was out cold.

'I know you're not Walter Lestrange, mister. You don't fool me. You're a peace officer an' no mistake. And for you, this is the end of the road. You've done all the investigating for this trip, and for any other, come to that!'

Sam was quite clearly unconscious by this time. The talking ceased, and instead, the masked fellow went into action again. He backtracked into the other cellar and came back with a can of paraffin. This he uncorked and poured out in a long stream across the floor just inside the joining arch.

As soon as he had finished his deadly work, he produced from his pocket a match, which he rasped on his thumb nail before applying to the trail of paraffin. The liquid was ignited with a slow roar. For extra measure, he tossed down the paraffin lamp which Sam had brought from reception.

Chuckling wickedly to himself, the masked man hurriedly withdrew. The roar of the flames drowned the sound of his footsteps as he went up the stairs to the floor above. The door opened and closed and he was gone.

In the inner cellar, the wine racks were made of wooden struts. One of the racks was extremely close to the flames, and already discarded boxes were catching fire. The empty containers fizzed and roared with flames and gradually the gap between the conflagration and the fallen man narrowed.

The containers collapsed, and, in doing so, fell across the nearest of the racks, sending it up in flames. As the struts across the racks began to give way, so the bottles at the different levels slipped down and piled up on top of one another. Sam had stumbled upon somebody who did not want to be investigated, but in doing so he had put himself in a situation of great danger.

12

The time came when another throbbing in Sam's head became louder and more insistent than the one caused by the blow on the head. He tried opening his eyes, but at first it seemed to be a painful experience. His senses were slow to return. The throbbing came from beyond his own body. It was caused by the heat. Along with the oppressive heat came a smell. At first he wrinkled his nose without knowing what he was smelling. There was smoke, of course, but he had not this far associated it with imminent danger.

He sneezed and sniffed again, and then he knew what the second smell was. It was that of burning hair. His eyebrows were taking a beating from the nearest burning object, a wooden packing case. He blinked, opened his eyes and at once he threw up his arm to protect his face. With an effort he came to his knees, as he did so, a loud noise occurred behind him.

A bottle's contents had expanded and blown out the cork. The cork in question hit him in the back like a bullet, but it did not penetrate, of course. A cursory observation of the extent of the fire had him wriggling backwards, away from the containers, the nearest rack and the burning paraffin.

The felt brim of his pointed hat had also been singed. He rounded the end of the nearest block of racks and staggered back, thankful to be alive, and yet fearful for the immediate future. The roaring noise made him think twice about calling for help. No one would hear his voice above the holocaust.

Very soon now, people above stairs would get a whiff of smoke and some sort of an effort would be made to locate the fire and get it under control. But would the help come in time to assist Sam, or would he have to survive by his own efforts?

While he stood undecided, tying his handkerchief around his face for protection, another bottle disgorged its cork. And then several more bottles did the same. Every time a bottle emptied itself, the liquid did a little towards checking the flames. What a pity that hundreds of bottles at once couldn't explode and materially check the advance of the fire! But that was too much to hope for.

Another rack ignited at the end nearest the fire, and the one beside it began to disintegrate with alarming rapidity. Again the bottles began to subside, but Sam did not wait to watch them. He was looking around for some means of helping himself. What in the world could he use for purposes of firefighting?

A block of wine racks collapsed, and the burning debris swept across the archway by which he would have to make his escape. He thought he could hear voices now, but the din of the fire made it difficult for him to be sure. Involuntarily, he backed another pace and he stumbled over something which gave him an idea.

He had fallen over a ramp, at the top of which was a huge beer barrel delicately poised. For the first time, he had a slight feeling of hope. If he could get the contents of the barrel, and maybe other barrels, near to the conflagration, then he would be able to fight the fire with a liquid of sorts. It was worth taking a chance over.

The barrel in question held many gallons, but he did not hesitate to make an effort to move it. It had to be turned through a quarter circle to get it in the direction necessary to roll it down the ramp. He searched around some more, and his foot encountered a small axe. He gripped it and the feel of it gave him confidence. He used it as a small lever, at the same time throwing his weight against the barrel.

The second time he tried there was a

creak and a groan and the barrel turned about six inches. The perspiration dripped off his forehead and down his face into the kerchief. Whirling smoke teased his nostrils. Any man would have given in, had he weakened at that moment, but the instinct to survive was a strong one.

He battled on, and succeeded in turning the barrel through a similar arc. After that a small amount of digging and probing with the axe blade was sufficient to put the article into line for a run down the slope. He coaxed it forward and jumped well clear, desperately anxious to see what effect it would have upon the burning racks directly opposite the archway.

Down it went, gathering momentum. There was a small bounce as it hit the floor, and then it went on again, side-swiping bottles which had rolled out of the racks. Into the pulsing smoky mass of burning it plunged, causing a sudden roar. The air was full of small flying fragments of burning wood and other material as the racks in its path collapsed and dropped their contents.

Corks were popping like the discharge of gatling guns, but the barrel had come to rest, and, perversely, its contents had remained intact. Sam ran after it, attacking the end which was nearer to him with the blade of the axe. After several hefty swings which dug in the blade, a section of timber gave way and the contents began to spill out.

The blade was still buried in the woodwork, and while it was in that position, Sam used it again as a lever and swung the whole object over so that the beer poured onto the centre of the burning area. Vapour went up like steam and the actual flames died down somewhat.

Sam backed off a couple of yards and watched what happened. The fire had definitely receded in front of the archway, and the timbers of the barrel were slow to ignite. Acting upon impulse, he took a run at the barrel, planted a foot upon it and heaved with all his strength.

At first he thought that his foot was going to slip off, but his leg held in the position in which it had landed and the barrel slowly rolled over hot bottles until it was through the archway and bumping into something beyond.

This, Sam believed, was the time to take a chance. He pulled his borrowed hat low down over his face, adjusted the handkerchief across the lower half, and plunged forward with his nerves jumping. Bottles slipped this way and that from under his feet, but he managed to stay upright, and to go through the archway which the disappearing barrel had proved was still there.

On the very edge of the smoke, which had very largely penetrated the outer cellar, he went head first over the top of the stationary barrel and banged his head on another solid rack. He winced, rose to his feet and collided with the figure of West, the manager, who was down there in his shirt sleeves, hugging the metal end of a hose pipe, which this far had not squirted any water.

'Lestrange! How in tarnation did you come to be in the middle of all that burnin'?'

Sam gripped him by the shoulder in a manner which showed he was glad to meet up with the manager in the cellar. 'It's a long story, West, an' I'd like to tell it later. You're goin' to lose your stock of wines and beer, but the fire will be contained to this level if you work hard with the hoses. I suppose you've got others besides these?'

West nodded and pushed him towards the staircase. On the way up, Sam had to undergo the startled and the curious glances of no less than four men of the town, who were among the volunteers for the town fire brigade.

In the foyer, he paused long enough to advise the town marshal and a few other local officials as to the extent of the fire, and then he went up to his room and threw himself on the bed. His action in going up to the room so soon after many others had evacuated theirs gave confidence to the workers, and those who sought to get the fire squad working.

Two hoses were run down the staircase, and a third was put down the shaft where the wine lift had operated. Within ten minutes the fire-fighters had water running through them, and the fire at once began to give ground.

Men swarmed down into the outer cellar and a chain of buckets were passed down to them. In a little over an hour, the worst was over and only flaming wooden embers gave cause for concern. The bottles had ceased to pop and three barrels of beer had been saved.

★   ★   ★

At four o'clock, Wilbur West retired to his private office with three bottles of warm white wine under his arm and the town marshal at his back. John Coltman, the marshal, had personally headed the group which had fought the blaze and he had done a good job. In his middle forties, he had held office in East Halt for the past four years.

He was a tall man with a ramrod straight back acquired at an earlier age while serving as a junior officer in the Confederacy cavalry. It said a lot for his ability and his personality that he was in office at a time when a lot of other men with a similar record were steadfastly kept out of official appointments.

In appearance he looked a strong character. His well-groomed brown hair and military moustache combined with his small Roman nose to make him look a very positive individual. He sat down with care in the visitor's chair and held his hands rather carefully, having suffered many small superficial burns.

'Pour me a glass, Wilbur and pour it fast. It will do jest anyhow so long as it ain't boiling.'

The hotel manager obliged, pouring for both of them. Marshal Coltman drained his glass and held it out for more, which he received without delay. After wiping his moustache rather gingerly, the peace officer opened up a discussion.

'What I still need to know is how it all started. It was the quiet time of the afternoon. These conflagrations don't start themselves, Wilbur. Somebody has to do something a little bit stupid. Now, who on earth did you have go down there to get something? You'll know the answer to that question by now.'

West nodded. His face was streaked with smoke, but he did not seem to mind. 'So far as I know, nobody went down to get anything. The only fellow who went below was one who called on me this morning. Name of Walter Lestrange. He had a card with him. Apparently he has the right to check the wine stocks and so on. A descendant of the founder, Charles Holborn.'

'Lestrange must have knocked over the lamp, or somesuch. Anyways, he was the fellow I bumped into jest as I got below with the end of the first hose.

Those fine fair brows of his were burned another colour. In fact, there wasn't much of them left.'

West would have said more, but Coltman, sounding suspicious, interrupted him.

'His *fair* eyebrows, you were saying? Describe to me this Lestrange character, Wilbur. I'm a mite puzzled.'

'Well, he's a tall fair young hombre with wavy hair and freckles. He has green eyes an' he's cleanshaven. Shall I go on?'

'No need to bother, old friend. The man you are describin' was not Walter Lestrange. Lestrange has black hair, sideburns. There could not be any mistake.'

A quiet knock on the door preceded the arrival of Sam Regan, who nodded and stepped inside with a quiet air of confidence. He had removed the scorched clothing which had belonged to Lestrange and was now wearing his own outfit. The green shirt, white bandanna and brown leather vest. And the stetson with the flat crown and pointed brim was also his own. He took it off, and found himself an upright chair which he sat on.

He began: 'Gentlemen, I believe I owe the pair of you an explanation. It was good I found you both here together.'

Neither of his hearers spoke. He cleared his throat and pulled out from his pocket his badge of office, dangling it where they could clearly see it.

'I'm Sam Regan, deputy sheriff, workin' out of the office of Moses Wallis in the county seat. I came along here and masqueraded as Walter Lestrange because I thought it would help me in my enquiries into the bank raid at the Bankers' Hotel in Blackwood. I felt there was a tie-up between the outlaws and the Holborn hotels.'

West and Marshal Coltman regarded each other steadily. Clearly neither of them doubted Sam's identity, now that he had made it clear who he was and why he had used another man's identity. But there were things which puzzled them, and they hesitated who should ask first.

West remarked: 'You were takin' your duties mighty serious in checkin' the hotel cellars, Sam. What did you hope to gain by that, an' what in tarnation did you do to start the fire? You were lucky to survive!'

'I was searchin' the cellars because I thought I might find something down there which had nothin' to do with wines. A secret hoard of some sort. It isn't generally known but the loot from the last bank raid was hidden for a while in the cellars under the hotel.

'As for the fire itself, I didn't start it. That was done by an enemy. A man I was on the lookout for. He hit me with something hard, an' while I was unconscious he poured paraffin along the floor and then set fire to it. The lamp was thrown down for extra measure. As you pointed out, I was lucky to survive.'

John Coltman was stroking his

moustache with his right hand. He said: 'Whatever happened to Walter Lestrange, Sam?'

'He was shot by renegades in the west of the county and buried earlier this week over in Great Wells. He found the money in the cellar under the Bankers' Hotel. That was why they shot him. I'm sorry about him, in a way. He wasn't a bad fellow. He merely gave way to temptation when the chance of a lot of money came his way.'

Sam went into detail how Lestrange had been attacked and told of subsequent developments. His listeners were impressed when they heard the part he had played. West offered him a glass of wine, which he took with gratitude.

'What can we do for you now, then?' the manager asked.

'Muster the regular men on your payroll and let us see if we can find my attacker. You'll remember I looked through a staff list earlier. Well, I drew a blank. I can only think that the man who came after me had joined you under an alias. After raising a fire, he may have quit your employment without notice.'

In five minutes, West had mustered the staff. They consisted of three men and five women. On this occasion, a man named Eddie Curtiss appeared to be missing. Moreover, Eddie Curtiss had blue-black kinky hair of the type seen on the fire-raiser.

13

As soon as it was ascertained that Curtiss was nowhere in the hotel, the rest of the staff were dismissed again and sent about their everyday duties.

Wilbur West led the town marshal and Sam Regan up to the third floor where the man believed to be Ezekiel Carver had had his room. It was a small pokey affair with a dormer window opening out onto the rear.

The occupant had hastily packed his gear, leaving behind a necktie and an old vest. Two old newspapers were lying about, one of which had an account of the bank raid in Blackwood. In one of the drawers of the dressing chest, the fellow had left behind a small tintype photograph of himself in a round pillbox hat and wearing a small bolero. The photograph was signed *Yours very sincerely, Zeke.*

The searchers gave it from one to another. Sam said, 'I guess that's all the confirmation I need. That's our man, the one you knew as Eddie Curtiss. I was told his name was Ezekiel or Zeke Carver. And there he's signed the name of Zeke. I guess he's one man I'd dearly like to meet up with again.'

Coltman, who had parked his big frame near the window, coughed, and shook his head. 'For a criminal that was mighty careless, leavin' the picture lyin' about. I don't reckon he's likely to have left anything else of value, though.'

This last remark was prompted because Sam was on his hands and knees, looking under the threadbare mat in the middle of the room. While he searched around the floor, West, who was clearly trying to be helpful, stripped the bed and examined the mattress. That particular bit of the search yielded nothing. Obviously Carver was not a man to secrete his treasures around the bed.

Coltman studied a shelf above the

clothes alcove and Sam carried his part of the search into every corner of the room. They were on the point of giving up when Sam went over to the wash hand stand and bent down once again. He felt underneath, and his probing hand came into contact with paper fastened to the underside.

In an instant, he had gone down on one knee and peered underneath. He brought out his knife and carefully separated the folded paper from the wooden frame on the underside. West shifted the big water jug out of the way and the three of them bent over the paper which Sam was quick to straighten out.

It was done in ink, in the form of a plan. Sam caught sight of two words in block letters, and his spirits at once rose. He whistled.

He said: 'Gents, I believe we've struck pay dirt. Let's take this document along to the office and put a lamp over the top of it. Judgin' by what I can see, 'hotel' and 'Junction,' this might jest possibly have something to do with the outlaws' next port of call.'

On the big desk, with the lamp lit over it, the plan looked even more significant. Prominent in the middle of the plan was a big square building clearly marked 'H. Hotel, Junction.' Junction being the name of the next settlement further north than East Halt. Junction was about the same distance as East Halt from the county seat, but in direction it was east-north-east.

The hotel's foyer on the corner of Main Street and an intersection was clearly shown. So was the manager's office in the first floor. This was on the west side of the building, overlooking an alleyway which separated the hotel from an office block right next door. Sam was intrigued to note that the office safe front had been shown in the plan, as well as the spot where the manager had his desk, and where the door was located.

The alleyway to the north was also

shown, separating the hotel from a large rooming house. On the right of the intersection, and matching the hotel for frontage, was the Junction Saloon. As they pored over the plan, giving it their full attention, the trio were distracted from the immense setbacks of that afternoon, and pitchforked by their discovery into the immediate future.

After a while, they all sat back and smoked. They had the feeling that the discovery was almost too good to be true.

'So they were aimin' to hit the Holborn Hotel in Junction,' Coltman remarked. 'Now that they've lost the plans they'll never carry it through. It would be too risky. No criminal would have the nerve to go through with it, if he thought his plans were rumbled.'

'I still think they might,' Sam argued. 'After all, it was only a bit of luck that I managed to find the plan in the first place. It might have been there for years, undiscovered. And if anyone else had found it, they would probably have thrown it away, not knowing what it was all about. No, I think I must act on what has been discovered today, an' I'd be obliged if you two gents don't mention a word about it. Otherwise, the advantage which we have might become negative.'

Coltman and West were quick to agree that it should be kept a secret. They had suggestions to make, as well.

'You'll need to alert the peace officers in the town as soon as possible,' the marshal pointed out.

'And as you don't know when this strike is likely to be made you won't have to waste any time in getting things organized to stop them,' West added.

'Your advice is good, gents,' Sam admitted. 'It is my intention to send one or two cryptic telegraph messages to the county seat, an' then head for Junction myself first thing in the morning.'

★　★　★

In a small dugout cabin built into a hillside a short distance to the north-east of East Halt, four men were playing a game of cards during the afternoon of the following day. The top of the table had not been finished very smoothly, and two of the wooden stools on which they were sitting had uneven legs, making it necessary for the card players to push the legs well into the earth floor to get an even balance.

The building had only one window and one door, and yet it was considered by the men who used it to be almost an ideal hideout.

They were an ill-assorted quartette. At forty, Zeke Carver was the oldest man present. He played confidently, a stiff-built dominating character with dark, brooding eyes and black wavy hair worn close to the skull. As he played he toyed with his closely-trimmed mous-tache and occasionally scratched his chest through his thick plaid shirt.

On Carver's right was Red Hutton, a bulky man in his late twenties with carrotty red hair and heavy features. He played slowly and very deliberately, clad in a sweat-stained khaki shirt and an undented stetson which was pushed back off his bony forehead.

To Carver's left, Bummer Spence was playing with great confidence. He was a tall, big-boned man with flat features and no eyebrows. In colouring, he was fair. In contrast, he wore a black outfit.

The fourth member of the team was the smallest. He was a Mexican by birth. He had close-cut black hair, a slight squint, and the inevitable steeple hat of his race.

All four men carried a brace of guns apiece, and their belt knives had a finer edge on them than those carried by most Westerners. Tobacco smoke rose from the tips of four home-rolled cigarettes. Two candles added to the daylight provided by slanting sun rays.

Spence, who had just won a hand, gathered to him the coin money stacked in the middle of the table, while Carver took it upon himself to pick up the cards and give them a shuffle.

Carver yawned. Hutton and Sonora glowered at Spence, and the latter spoke the thoughts of all of them.

'I wonder how much longer the Boss is goin' to be?'

'Not very long,' Carver surmised. 'I guess he must have called in at East Halt on the way to look at the damage to the hotel.'

His cronies eyed him significantly. They admired his complete ruthlessness when he thought that anything had to be done. Nothing at all was ever allowed to stand in his way.

'Do you think the Boss will be displeased about the fire at the hotel?' Bummer wanted to know.

Carver seemed surprised. 'No, why should he? It isn't as if he owns any of the Holborn hotels. He jest happens to be one of the longest servin' managers, that's all. He has no cause to beef about what I did back there. After all, I had happened upon a prowler, an' for certain sure he was a peace officer.'

'Jest the same, it'll be interestin' to see what sort of an attitude he takes to the latest goings on,' Bummer persisted.

Carver shared out the cards and another game was started. Ten minutes later, Sonora tossed down his cards and rushed to the window. He had heard the sounds of a horse approaching. Presently, the others joined him, their game forgotten for the time being.

A hefty-looking man on a chestnut gelding was coming up the draw and heading straight for them. There was no cause for alarm, however, for this was none other than Mark Durbin, manager of the Holborn Hotel in South Creek, and the real leader of the assembled gang of outlaws.

Durbin was thirty-four years of age, a prosperous man with fair wavy hair and bushy sideburns. He was dressed in a derby hat, and a jacket and trousers of brown corduroy. His bulbous eyes were set unblinkingly upon the window and his jaw and mouth were rather grimly posed. He carried only one hand gun.

Durbin dismounted and slackened the saddle of his horse, while his subordinates came out and gathered around him. He managed a grin before his eyes settled on Zeke Carver.

'Howdy, boys. Zeke, that sure was a spectacular thing you did in the cellar of the East Halt hotel. All that to get rid of an inquisitive peace officer. He got away an' all you did was burn up the fixtures and fittings. He used the wine and the beer to help dowse the flames while he made his escape. As near as I can tell, he's a deputy of some sort from the county seat. Probably the jasper who shot Roscoe the other day. Let's get indoors now an' get down to business.'

Sonora gave up his stool to Durbin, and instead sat upon an old packing case. Durbin studied the cards on the table. Red brought him a mug of coffee from the stove, and he eyed each of them in turn. Without comment, he started to fumble in the pockets of his corduroy jacket. One after another, he produced four separate wads of currency notes of high denomination. Each was put down in front of a man.

The faces of the quartette broke out into cheery grins. Durbin then produced a box of cigars and placed it in the middle of the table. One after another, they took one, lighting it from their cigarettes.

'Boys, I hope you've all got a safe place in which to keep that money, because you don't want to spend it in a hurry. Right now, we're goin' into details about our next little job, an' that will mean more treasury notes to spend. So let's get to business.'

Durbin took off his derby and hung it on a hook behind the door. It was a signal for the discussion to begin.

He resumed: 'You'll all know that we plan to hit the Holborn Hotel in Junction, an' you might like to know why. The fact is, Ellis Montford, the manager in Junction, don't use the bank as often as he ought to do. He's efficient, but not a particularly good businessman. He spends too much time entertaining the important guests in the private saloon with that guitar of his.'

'What sort if a man is he?' Hutton asked, his brow puckered.

Durbin glanced across at Carver, who took up the talking.

'Montford? He's a dark, dapper man with a goatee beard. Smartly dressed in tailored suits, most of the time. What we plan to do is extract the loot silently from the safe in Montford's office while he's out having a meal with the Boss, here.

'I meant to bring along with me a plan of the hotel in Junction but unfortunately I left the last spot in a hurry, so I'll have to talk without it. Montford's office is on the first floor. It has a window which opens onto the alley which separates the hotel from the office block further up the street.

'What we plan to do is drop the cash down into the alley and have it picked up by one of you boys, who will be actin' as a guard an' lookout down there. There's practically nothing to go wrong. You, Sonora, will be watchin' the horses across the street. Red will be patrolling the alley on the north side of the building, and you, Bummer, will be hangin' around the foyer an' the intersection. The plan is foolproof. The Boss and I could pull the job between us. The rest of you are only there to offset the unexpected.'

Durbin pointed his cigar at Carver. 'Tell the boys how you plan to get the money out of the safe without makin' any noise, Zeke.'

Carver grinned. 'I'm goin' to take an impression of the key to the safe. Montford leaves it hanging up in his office for long periods when he's indoors. Soap is the thing for the impression, an' I have a metal blank ready to file down to the correct size.'

There was a short pause, which seemed to indicate that Durbin was satisfied with Carver's deliberations. He made no mention of the hotel plans which had failed to reach this planning stage.

'What happens if someone turns up right when you are busy at the safe?' Sonora queried quietly.

Carver removed his cigar rather slowly. 'Then I don't panic. I do what I can to remove the opposition without noise. If there is any shootin' then I try to get the loot out through the window, the same as we planned. I'll expect help from Bummer and Red.'

'We'll leave town by the south-east route, and eventually make our way back here. The only thing we haven't fixed so far, is the date an' the time.'

All eyes turned to Mark Durbin for these details. He rolled his cigar around his mouth, but did not trouble to remove it.

'The strike will be made around two o'clock the day after tomorrow. I want you boys to get plenty of sleep so that you'll be fit an' alert for what lies ahead of you. *Comprende*?'

Everyone approved this course of action.

14

Ellis Montford, the manager of the Holborn Hotel in Junction, Basin County, had been associated with the town for many years. He had arrived there as a young man with a group of travelling theatrical people and decided that his days of travelling were over.

His first break was when a local man offered him the managership of a big saloon, and from that useful beginning he had branched out as the custodian of the leading hotel. All his life, he had been interested in music in an amateur sort of way. He had managed to master the Spanish guitar, and now, on what was to be one of the critical days of his working life, he was practising at eleven o'clock in the morning in his private suite on the first floor.

He did not look his fifty years. His goatee beard was still jet black. He was well dressed in a maroon buttoned vest, a white shirt and string tie and a lightweight grey smoking jacket. He had kept a good growth of hair on the crown of his head. Now, only a very few silver hairs gave the hint to his real age.

The man who came up to his door and listened, Mark Durbin, from another hotel in the same chain, was surprised to hear the sounds of a bow scraping across a violin, instead of the gentle strumming sound of the guitar, which he had expected.

Durbin gave a gentle knock. At first, the manager, who had given instructions to his own staff not to disturb him, ignored the knocking. Durbin, however, was persistent. He knocked again, and this time the bowing exercises stopped and a light footstep approached the door.

The sunburnt brow was furrowed and angry as the face appeared, but as soon as Montford saw Durbin standing there with his hat in his hand, the dapper musician's whole expression changed.

'Why, Mark, Mark Durbin, how nice to see you in town, and how pleasant to have a visit from you!'

Montford glanced rather guiltily at the violin in his right hand, and Durbin, who knew how to humour him, pointed to it and gave out with an expression of surprise.

'Shucks, it sure is good to be right here in little old Junction, an' to know that your domain is still prosperin', Ellis, but I can see you're practisin'. I know how important it is to you to get in your regular practice. Especially when you are workin' on an unfamiliar instrument. I'd like to talk to you, but I won't stay now. How would it be if the two of us met for a late lunch, at, say, two o'clock right here in the hotel?'

Montford beamed. 'Very well, then, Mark, it's a date. I'll get on with my scrapin' of the fiddle while you attend to any outstandin' business you have. See you at two o'clock, as you suggest, in the dinin' room. At my private table. Adios, amigo.'

Durbin grinned, in his turn. 'Till two o'clock, old friend.' He turned on his heel, returned to the staircase, and went down below again. On the way out, he called in at the small smoking room on the ground floor. There, he purchased a few long cigars. He lit one before he left the building, and then strolled gently out into the fresh air.

For nearly five minutes, he stood casually gazing across at the mercantile store and the saddler's shop where Senora was going to tether the horses for use in a case of emergency. He recollected that he was actually standing in the spot where Bummer Spence would be keeping his vigil, and that Zeke Carver was already in the hotel, occupying a room not very far from Ellis Montford's private suite.

Presently, he strolled out of the foyer and made a tour of the building. His eyes were very much on the alert as he moved up the alley on the west side, under the window of the manager's office, where the safe was located. He noted that there was a window in an office in the next building directly opposite the window of Montford's office. The window in question, however, was streaked with dirt, a sure indication that the office was not occupied. This realization pleased him. He moved on again, came to the backs, and turned eastward along the northern perimeter of the hotel. This was the area where Red Hutton would patrol, until such time as the loot was dropped from the window.

Soon, he had made the circuit, and he felt reasonably satisfied that nothing could go wrong with the plan, which would be implemented a few hours later. Having thus satisfied himself, he wandered off in a westerly direction in search of something to distract him.

The plans of the opposition had also gone through the early stages. Sam Regan had interviewed Marshal Tom Ferris that morning at a little after seven o'clock. Sam was gambling that this day was most likely to be the one for the strike against the hotel.

Consequently, the forces of law and order were out in force, but secretly. No less than a dozen riders, in groups of three, were idling about to north, south, east and west of town, waiting for a concerted rush in any of the four directions by disconcerted outlaws. Each of these men had been sworn to secrecy before being deputized for the job of helping to keep the peace.

Tom Ferris, who did not want any knowledge of his plans to be leaked abroad, had perforce to stay in his office and act as if everything was normal. In age, Ferris was fifty, the same as Ellis Montford, but his appearance made him look many years older. His straggling grey moustache and white hair, combined with a stoop, gave the impression that he was far past his best, whereas, in actual fact, he was quite active, and as good in a saddle as he had ever been. His eye, also, was as keen as when he was in his physical prime, and many a wrongdoer who hopefully went for his gun had found himself to be outdrawn for speed in the past decade.

Ferris chewed tobacco and stared gloomily out of his office window, wondering when the attack would come, and how it would develop when it did take place. The waiting was getting him down long before midday.

* * *

Long before the time when Mark Durbin strolled around the outside of the hotel, Sam Regan had gone to earth in the first floor office across the alley from the office of the hotel manager. He had a low camp bed in there, and he spent most of his time reclining upon that, taking care to keep his body well below the eyeline of anyone looking up from the alley and from the building next door.

In order to pass the time, Sam had

taken in with him a full sack of Bull Durham tobacco and plenty of cigarette papers. He had the door of his room slightly ajar, and the lower of the two windows had a gap under it of two inches. He did not think that an observer would notice that it was open.

While he waited, he did without food and simply fed his mind on anything that occurred to him. Very largely, his thoughts ranged over the happenings of what he was coming to think of as the fateful days. The days, in fact, since the raid on the Bankers' Hotel, and all subsequent events. He had the feeling that he was the victim of circumstances, and that his circumstances now could only change for the better.

He regretted the day that his job had made it necessary for him to shoot down a boyhood friend. He also regretted having lost the friendship of that young man's parents and the affection of his sister. Nothing, in his present opinion, could ever be the same.

All he could do was work at this case to vindicate his earlier actions. Life certainly seemed to have handed him a raw deal.

Around one o'clock, Sam grew tired of the taste of nicotine. He rubbed out a half smoked cigarette on the side of the wooden ladder which he had in the room with him. In spite of all his efforts, within a few minutes he had dozed off to sleep.

* * *

At five minutes to two o'clock, Mark Durbin reappeared in the foyer of the Holborn Hotel. At once, Ellis Montford stepped from behind the reception counter, came forward and shook him by the hand. Side by side, and talking in a cordial fashion, they strolled off to the dining room and settled down at the table which the resident manager kept for himself.

Sonora was in place across the street, putting on an act of boredom while he seemed to await a friend. The Mexican horse-minder gave a special signal to Bummer Spence who was up the intersection, idling in front of the Junction saloon on the opposite side from the hotel.

Bummer showed no special hurry. He, in his turn, signalled to Red Hutton who was lounging on the mouth of the alley on the north side of the hotel. Red wandered out of view, and Bummer sauntered across the street and continued his time-wasting near the foyer.

High in the building, Zeke Carver had also seen Bummer's signal. Carver was the key man, and he at once set off for the manager's office, taking great care not to let anyone see him actually approach it.

The door was a loose fitting one, and the lock responded almost at once to the piece of wire which he inserted in it. A moment later, he was inside and standing against the back of it, breathing deeply with the excitement of what he was doing.

He fumbled in his pocket and brought out the key which he had fashioned specially for the purposes of this robbery. He was hoping that this one would be the first entirely quiet operation in which he had taken part. In fact, he saw silent robbery as being a cut above the other, more noisy operations.

Whistling soundlessly to himself, he crossed to the window and looked out. When he was sure that he was not observed, he lifted the lower half of the window and raised it, leaving a gap of a couple of feet. In doing so, he caused the window to creak, and that was just sufficient noise to disturb the sleeper in the office across the way.

★ ★ ★

Sam was hatless and perspiring. Some of his perspiration was not occasioned by the heat. He was in the throes of a daytime nightmare brought on by his pondering over recent troubles before going off to sleep.

In his nightmare he was pinned down, probably held by a rope, to a narrow camp bed. His room was some sort of a prison. There was one person in the room with him, and that, when the person turned her head, turned out to be Mirabelle.

He could see the swish of her hair and the glint in her eye as though she were really there, just a yard or so away from him. In her hand, she had a Colt revolver. The weapon she held was diabolically steady. She advanced slowly with it held in front of her and pointed it at his chest.

What caused most of his perspiration to start out from his forehead was the way in which he could see her finger curl around the trigger.

He was protesting: 'No, Mirabelle, don't shoot. You'll regret it! You'll have to live with the shootin' for the rest of your life!'

And Mirabelle was replying: 'Your advice is no doubt good, Sam, because you ought to know what it is like to kill a man. You killed my brother, an' now you have to live with the guilt of it for the rest of your life.'

She smiled and leaned towards him. 'But I'm going to do you a favour. I'm goin' to avenge the Arnott family honour by shootin' you in turn. I hope you sweat in hell!'

As she was about to pull the trigger, he lurched off his camp bed and found himself lying prone across the wooden ladder laid along the floor. He blinked the salt perspiration out of his eyes and looked around, first over one shoulder and then over the other. It seemed absolutely unreal at first when he discovered that he was alone with the door closed.

Gradually, he returned to normality and to a proper idea of what was going on. He realized that something a little bit unusual must have cut in upon his nightmare and he looked round for the most likely thing to have done it.

It was not until he glanced out of the

window that he saw what must have roused him. The lower half of the window of Montford's office had been pushed up. At once, he withdrew and only looked again when he was sure that he could not be seen. There was no one in the alley, but he could imagine what might be going on in the hotel manager's office.

If the thief at the safe was already busy, then there was no time to waste. Sam eased up his own window, and by placing his head near to the sill, he was just able to detect furtive moments across the alley in the other room.

Now was the time to put his simple plan into operation. Whether it would work or not would soon become apparent. He picked up from the floor a firecracker; the type which banged and spluttered several times in succession when lit. There was a small stone attached to it, to help him with his aim.

As soon as the cracker was spluttering he moved again to the window, and this time he leaned out. Entirely unobserved, he swung the small object through an arc and then let go of it. It curved through the air of the passageway and gently flopped through the window opposite. Almost at once, the first explosive crack was heard. Then it did the same again. A man gave a cry of annoyance, and tried to stamp it out, but the maker had done his job well and the cracker continued to bang.

Meanwhile, Sam, who was keeping well down out of sight, took a hold of his ladder and hauled it to the window. He put one end on the sill, and began to push it through, into the open air. About two rungs at a time, he made substantial progress with it, gradually bridging the gap between the two buildings.

When half of it was out of the window it became a little more difficult to handle. Sam swung on the back end of it and heaved again. The outside end banged against the wall opposite and that was a warning for him to get back to the window and guide it more carefully. To set the outer end firmly on the window sill opposite required a few seconds of close concentration.

He achieved this, but as the top of the ladder banged down into the required place, Zeke Carver appeared just behind it with a revolver in his hand. He fired it without the slightest hesitation, and the bullet went close enough to singe the cloth of Sam's shirt sleeve.

15

As the bullet ripped into the woodwork behind him, Sam dropped to the floor, putting himself out of sight. He noted the singe mark on his sleeve, shrugged over it and at once pulled his own right-handed Colt. He crawled away from the window, and rounded the end of the ladder.

His head came up and he saw a movement at the other end of the ladder. Carver, as yet unidentified, was moving around, looking for a target. Without hesitation, Sam fired back, twice. His quarry went out of sight, and that seemed like a good time to start moving out along the ladder.

As his head and shoulders emerged from the window, he could have wished that the ladder was lashed down, but that was too much to hope for. If he dallied too long, the intruder and his accomplices might very well abandon the hotel before the forces of law and order could make any sort of a move against them. This was the last thing that Sam wanted to happen.

He was personally committed to make the first move against the intruder in the office, and he went ahead without hesitation. The rungs of the ladder were hard on his knees, but he kept on moving, and soon he was half way across the gap.

A slight breeze tugged at his bandanna and gave him a touch of vertigo as the contraption moved under him. This far, there had been no sign of the intruder. Nothing to show that he was still active, or, for that matter, still in the office.

The next move took Sam by surprise. From the north corner of the hotel, the head and shoulders of a bulky man in a khaki shirt suddenly appeared. The lower part of the face was concealed by a faded bandanna and a revolver was held with the muzzle pointing in Sam's direction. This observer, Red Hutton, was slow to take in the situation, but having heard the earlier gunshots and seen the star pinned to Sam's shirt he decided to play a part in the exchanges.

He rested his weapon upon his left forearm, panned it around in search of the target and fired a shot aimed at the body. Sam was in a bad position, particularly as he was concentrating upon the window in front of him to the exclusion of all else.

The bullet hit a side of the ladder and was deflected, missing the crawling man. In a flash, Sam had drawn his own weapon again and fired back. Two bullets chipped wood out of the corner of the wall behind which Hutton had withdrawn.

Sam waited, his gun poised and the muscles of his stomach knotting up. Again, he was taken by surprise. Carver, in the room ahead of him, contrived to keep low, and at the same time to push the end of the ladder back off the sill with a strong wooden lever.

In a matter of seconds, Sam was dropping down through the air, now firmly gripping the two sides of the ladder. Behind and above him, the window through which he had emerged was demolished by the rear end of the ladder. Glass fragments of wood spilled down into the alley, but not before the other end of the ladder had hit the earth and loosened Sam's precarious hold.

He contrived to tuck in his head, but his shoulders hit the hard earth of the alley floor with a good deal of force. The jolt left him half stunned and rolling into a prone position. He was facing the rear end when Red Hutton reappeared with both guns in his fists. Obviously, this time the outlaw thought he had the advantage, but Sam's gun had fallen close to his outstretched hand, and he at once gripped it and aimed it at the crouching figure.

All he was able to accomplish before his senses slipped away from him was the firing of one shot. His aim was on the low side, but it was effective. Hutton was hit in the thigh, and he collapsed almost at once with his guns unfired. From that moment forward, the wounded outlaw's only aim was to get away from the spot which was steadily becoming more unhealthy.

Dragging himself a few inches at a time, he moved out of the alley where the action had been and turned the corner into the other one. Meanwhile, Sam's cheek slumped into the dust and he lay unconscious with his gun still to hand and swirling smoke.

★ ★ ★

Almost at once, two or three galloping horses began to come down the main thoroughfare. It was the sound of mounted men approaching, on top of the surprise which Sam had occasioned, which made the other watchers panic.

Bummer, without a bandanna on his

face and trying to look as inconspicuous as possible, made a short trip to the street end of the alley and saw all the confirmation he needed to know that something serious had gone wrong.

No money bag. A man with a deputy's badge unconscious on the floor and Red Hutton nowhere to be seen. He glanced up to see if Carver was at the window, but saw nothing to reassure him. At his back, the horses were still advancing and men here and there were beginning to shout. No one this far knew exactly where the source of the trouble was, but it was obvious to many in the vicinity that something untoward had happened.

Bummer glanced across at the diminutive figure of Sonora. The little Mexican was already in the saddle. He was almost motionless, his hands busy with a black cigar, but Bummer had known him long enough to know that he was about to pull out, alone, almost at once.

Having perceived the Mexican's

reactions, he knew what he wanted to do himself. He was now all for a getaway. It would be healthy to get clear of town in a hurry. And what was one raid which had failed? They still had the payout money from their last effort. But time was pressing. Making a small hand gesture, he crossed the street, released his own from the small bunch of riderless horses and swung into leather.

Three riders were less than thirty yards away when Bummer and Sonora walked their horses around the first corner and then gave them a touch of the spurs. Off they went in a cloud of dust, to turn sharply down an alley into another street.

Their speed of departure, however, attracted some attention and soon the three deputized horsemen were following their trail and making a small amount of progress in the effort to overtake them.

★   ★   ★

No fewer than six horsemen were patrolling the perimeter of town in the south-east. A mere few minutes later, Sonora and Spence came bursting out of a street end with their mounts buffeting the dust out of the street surface.

A hoarse deputy bellowed out: 'Hold it right there!'

And that was the signal for Bummer to pull his twin guns and start taking potshots at the deputies. As he started shooting some of his nervousness left him, but his aim was not too good, and when one of the deputies returning his fire accidently shot the horse from under him, he tossed down his weapons and hurriedly hoisted his hands.

Sonora, meanwhile, had doubled back, but he had only succeeded in running into the three riders who were following. Having seen Bummer surrender, the Mexican did the same with a bad grace.

He was obliged to hand over his weapons, and to dismount and walk back towards the town marshal's office. The route which their captors took did not permit them another look at the outside of the hotel.

Because of this move they did not know that Carver had walked out by the ordinary door with the loot under his arm, and that he had hastily withdrawn, putting himself out of sight again.

* * *

Half an hour later, Pete Black, the town's bespectacled sawbones, had just finished bathing and padding Sam's cut and bruised shoulders. Sam was quick to get back into his shirt and to don his vest. He was fixing his white bandanna in place when the door opened and Marshal Tom Ferris took delivery of two outlaws, namely, Sonora and Bummer Spence.

These two were hurriedly placed together into a cell which was directly at the rear of the office. They looked a sullen, crestfallen pair as they squatted together on the hard wooden board which was theirs for a seat.

Sam's head was not as clear as it might have been, but he had been up to Montford's office before allowing anyone to bring him along to the peace office for treatment, and he knew that Carver had managed the robbery before making his escape. Ferris was clearly very pleased to have this pair in his cell, but Sam felt sure that they were only pawns in the game of robbery.

Red Hutton, the outlaw shot in the thigh, was also locked up, but his cell was through a door at a rear corner of the office and down a corridor which communicated with a small corral at the rear. Hutton's wound was such that he would not be walking about for a week or two.

Having dealt with Sam's needs, Doctor Black went back to the corridor cell and completed his work, putting on extra bandaging for better support. When he looked up, Sam was standing behind him, waiting to talk to the patient.

The doctor remarked: 'I know you have a job to do, Sam, an' that you need information, but this man really should not be questioned for long. Although he's a prisoner he ought to be given a bit of privacy after this. I'll call in and see him again late this evening. He may develop a fever.'

Sam managed a grin. 'All right, Doc, I won't keep him long. Jest a few questions an' then I'll feel like a rest myself. So long, Doc.'

Black nodded. He left the cell, turning the key in the lock and leaving it there. Sam went down on one knee beside Hutton, whose face was flushed.

He said: 'Howdy, I'm the man who shot Roscoe Lacey. I've been on your trail for some time. We were wise to your raid on the hotel in this town. You've collected trouble for yourself, an' no reward this trip. How would you like to do yourself a bit of good?'

Hutton, who was muffled up in extra blankets, merely shrugged his shoulders. He was starting to shiver. His condition was more or less as the doctor had predicted. He gestured for Sam to come closer. The latter did as he requested, thinking he wanted to whisper something of a significant nature.

'I — I could do with this camp bed further away from the cell window. I'm in a draught.'

Sam sighed, but he did what was required of him, hauling the camp bed away from the outer wall without bothering to call for help. He glanced up at the open bars. The current of air coming in through them was scarcely perceptible.

'Have you ever been in the penitentiary before?' he asked.

Hutton shook his head.

'In that case, you could get off with only a light sentence this time. That is, if I could say in court that you had done your best to help the sheriff's office by giving all information required of you.

'I know that a man named Zeke Carver is closely involved with this — this Creek Basin Gang, but it's my belief there's another man around who really gives the orders. If I knew the name of that man, or where to locate him, I'd be in a position to do you a whole lot of good. Now, what do you say?'

Hutton managed a sketchy grin. 'I could say that I'd dropped a coin in the alley behind the hotel, an' that I was lookin' for it when I saw a man climbing into the manager's office along a ladder. I fired at the jasper because I'm a law-abidin' sort of fellow, an' the intruder fired back at me. Later, I tried again to put a bullet in this hombre, who was a stranger to me. An' for my trouble I received a bullet in the leg.

'I wasn't to know you were a peace officer. You have to admit that it ain't every day a deputy sheriff crawls along a ladder in order to enter a man's private office!'

In spite of a general feeling of wariness, allied to his aches and pains recently acquired, Sam could just about see the humorous side of this situation. This fellow was actually putting up a verbal fight, and if no one else cracked, in some courts of law he might even be given the benefit of the doubt.

Gradually, Sam's mood changed. He said: 'I could put it around that you gave evidence that Zeke Carver was one of the leaders of the gang. That wouldn't do you any good, even if you managed to fool a whole court!'

Hearing this threat, Hutton flinched, a sure sign of fear. So Carver really was a man for his partners to be fearful of. The wounded man began to think he ought to say something, but he was not sure what sort of a statement it ought to be. To gain time, he asked: 'How did you come to know about Zeke Carver?'

Sam reached down for a glass of water, standing on the floor. As he did so, there was a change of sorts in the atmosphere of the cell. It was not clear at first what caused it, but Hutton suddenly sat up, in spite of his weakness. He was facing the open bars, fairly highly placed in the outer wall.

He shouted: 'No, Zeke! *No!*'

His words, however, were ignored. A head which Sam had seen before was up at the window. So was a long-barrelled wicked-looking hand gun. It was pointed at the chest of the man in the cot. Before Sam could react in any way, the gun had been steadied and fired. Two bullets transferred themselves from the cylinder to the chest of the wounded man, who promptly succumbed with a stricken look on his face.

Sam cursed himself for having left his gun belt in the main office. Carver, as ruthless and efficient as always, had withdrawn as soon as he had done what he came to do. He did not waste time and effort trying to gun down the prisoner's visitor. His interest for the moment did not run in that direction.

Having shot his victim to seal his lips forever, Carver withdrew, aiming to get clear of the rear of the building before the occupants came looking for him.

Sam ran out of the cell and up the corridor, heading for the office. There was no future in tearing out at the back without a gun. At the door which opened out from the office he collided rather heavily with Tom Ferris, who was on the way to join him. Sam had the worst of the collision. He sank to his knees, gasping out his explanation.

'Carver, out at the back! He's shot this man through the window!'

Roaring with frustration, Marshal Ferris turned on his heel and hurried through his office, going out by the front door and taking two other men after him.

Sam, meanwhile, staggered back to the cell. It was as well he did so without delay, for Hutton was still struggling to stay alive. After the last lethal event in his life, he was determined to say something worthwhile to the man who had interviewed him. Sam went down on his knees, first to examine him and then to listen.

Hutton said, on a fading whisper: 'The other man, the leader, his name is Mark Durbin, manager of the Holborn Hotel in South Creek. Got that? Mark Durbin! Go get him.'

Sam had not clearly heard the name the first time it was uttered, but the second time he heard it well. He waited for more, but Hutton's brief effort had left him spent. His eyes rolled and his head jerked. A minute later he was dead.

16

The first thing Sam did when he returned to the office was to buckle on his shooting iron. If he had had it with him a few minutes earlier, he might have shot Zeke Carver and saved the life of an unknown outlaw with red hair. But there was no use going into that now. He had before him two other members of the gang, and Tom Ferris, whose head was clearer, had gone out in pursuit of the killer.

Sonora and Spence were showing signs of agitation. The little man with the swarthy skin was gripping the bars, while the tall one was pacing up and down like a wild cat in a cage. Sam wondered if he could turn this situation to one of profit. They knew that something had happened down the corridor, but they did not know what. Sam had been so winded by Ferris that his voice did not carry to their cell.

For a minute or more, Sam listened hard for sounds coming from the rear of the building, but nothing happened. The killer and those who sought him had cleared out in a hurry. No one lurked at the back. The area was quiet.

Sam said: 'The redhead who was wounded in the alley is now dead.'

Spence joined his partner at the bars of the cell, gripping them a short distance above the Mexican's head.

'Who? Who did it? We have a right to know,' Spence blustered.

'He was shot in the chest from the window. One of your buddies did it. It was a premeditated, cold-blooded crime!'

Spence turned angrily to his partner. 'Don't take any notice of him, Sonora. As like as not he did the shooting himself!'

Bummer was glaring angrily in the direction of the deputy, who was squatting on the end of the desk. Sonora was looking up at his friend with troubled eyes. He was thinking that the deputy did not have a weapon when he went into the corridor to interrogate Hutton, and at the same time remembering the commotion round the back. The deputy could not have made that noise himself. Poor Bummer was trying hard to make the killing the work of the traditional enemy, the star toter, but he was not succeeding.

As Sam studied Spence's troubled face, his thoughts were hurriedly going back over what he had learned from the redhead. The leader of the gang was an important Holborn employee. In fact, the manager of the hotel in South Creek. According to the dying man, he had been the one to give the orders. Unfortunately, in learning what he had Sam had been the only witness to what had been said.

He found himself wondering if either of these two could be panicked into confirming what he already knew. It would be a good thing to have two live witnesses to corroborate the testimony of the dead man.

Rather belatedly, he remarked: 'I shot Roscoe Lacey, but I didn't have anything to do with the death of this redhead. The shootin' was done by your Boss! He must have thought that his liberty was about to be curtailed, that the redhead was about to name him as the boss renegade.'

Spence rasped a thumb nail around his jaw. His eyes were intently fixed on those of the deputy, who was maintaining a steady gaze, albeit with an effort. Sonora slowly shook his head, but he did not appear to be very convinced.

'If it wasn't Mark Durbin, then who do you think it was?' Sam queried bluntly.

A brief silence built up in the dusty room. The three men stood eyeing each other. Hostility was still in the air. Sam sat down again and toyed with his star. After a while, he spoke up again.

'I don't think Zeke Carver will get far this trip.'

The eyes of the prisoners looked away from him. They were acting in a cagey fashion, knowing he was trying to draw them out. Meanwhile, the tick of the clock on the wall appeared to grow more noisy.

Eventually, Bummer's mounting curiosity forced him to speak out.

'Where did you get that name? Gurbin or Burbin, or whatever it was?'

Sam grinned. 'You mean Mark Durbin? Oh, that's an easy one to answer. Your buddy in there named him before he died. What you boys ought to do, if you seek to get off lightly, is to confirm what your redheaded friend has already said. By the way, what *is* his name in there?'

Sam felt that if he could get them to say something, anything at all, it would be a start. Sonora was the one to oblige.

'You wouldn't kid us about him bein' dead, would you?'

Sam shook his head.

'Then the dead man's name is Red Hutton. He never did have an awful lot of luck in his life. And he didn't deserve to die the way he did. Tell us again what he said before he died!'

Sam was quick to oblige. 'He said that the leader's name was Mark Durbin, and that he was the manager of the Holborn Hotel in South Creek. I'm not likely to forget what he said in a hurry. All I want is your confirmation.'

Sonora was on the point of giving it, but Bummer's nature was a more suspicious one. He took more convincing of the true state of affairs. 'If we say what you want us to, it'll be a big help to you, won't it?'

Sam nodded, and moved a few feet towards them.

'In that case, let us see for ourselves that Red Hutton is really dead. Then, maybe, we'll do what you ask us.'

Sam was suddenly impatient. 'You act like all that has happened was a put up job. It went like I said. You're wastin' time over this. All the same, if you mean what you say, I'll go against the rules of this building and take you out of your cell. Hold on a minute.'

As he went to collect the keys from the ring on the wall, Sam's thoughts kept slipping away beyond the building. He could not help wondering how the chase after Carver was progressing. Carver, he thought, was a tough character to contend with. More formidable than any of these men who had already seen the inside of the cells.

Soon, the key was rattling in the lock and the door was swinging open. Sam stood back, gun in hand and a wary look in his eye.

'I hope you don't plan to give me any trouble. This office can do without any more corpses. You, Shorty, lead the way. The door to the corridor is not locked.'

One after another the prisoners passed through, with Sam close on their heels. The outlaws hastened their steps until they were at the barred door of the cell which contained the still figure. Neither of them ventured to go inside. The expression on the set face was sufficient to tell them all they needed to know.

As they turned away, Sam gestured towards the small window where the killer's head had appeared. This caused Bummer to beat his chest with his fists.

'All right, all right,' he protested, 'you don't have to spell it out for us. We can see how it happened. An' we'll keep our side of the bargain. You heard the truth when Red said that Mark Durbin was the leader of the gang. Ain't that so, Sonora?'

'*Si*, it is so. Mark Durbin was the man who gave all the orders. Zeke Carver had a lot to do with the plannin' but Durbin was really the Boss. After seein' what he did to poor Red, I feel relieved to give evidence against him. Now, let's get back to the cell. I don't like this corridor. It gives me the creeps.'

Sam led them through the communicating door. They had just entered the office when the street door opened and Ferris stepped through, followed by the two men who had gone out with him.

Ferris began: 'What in tarnation is goin' on in my office? Sam, I'll allow the sheriff's men have a lot of authority, but to take prisoners out of a cell in my office is a diabolical liberty. What got into your head to do it?'

Sam's eyes were shooting warning glances at the three new arrivals, as he escorted his men into the cell and prepared to give his explanation. It occurred to him that if Tom Ferris blurted out the truth about the recent killing that these two men might have a change of heart about signing a statement.

He slammed the door shut, and locked it, turning defiantly to his would-be critics. 'I had to convince these two men that their pardner was really dead. Otherwise they wouldn't have testified to the name of the gang leader. Get the idea?'

One of the deputized men, a shaggy bearded ex-miner, wanted to say something. 'If it's of any interest to you,

deputy, the man who did the shootin'
has given us the slip. It's one thing to
know the name of — '

'Hold on, amigo!'

Sam spoke in a loud angry voice
which had the effect of making the
speaker dry up. Marshal Ferris pointed
a gnarled forefinger at Sam, and opened
his mouth to speak. Again, Sam spoke
first.

'I know what I'm doin' don't seem all
that polite, Tom, but I think it's mighty
important for you not to blurt out
anything until these two prisoners have
signed a paper givin' the name of the
gang leader, Mark Durbin.'

Ferris mouthed the name of the
leader, Mark Durbin, but his lips
remained silent. The other deputized
man, a lean fellow with a big jaw, got as
far as : 'But that ain't — '

'Brother,' Sam cut in again, 'why
don't you mosey along to the nearest
eatin' house and fetch a whole big can
of coffee, sufficient for everybody here?'

By this time, Tom Ferris had a good

idea what was going on. He signalled for the speaker to do as Sam had suggested, and himself sat down in his chair and began to take paper from his desk.

He asked: 'What is this statement the prisoners are goin' to sign?'

Sam took off his hat and ran his fingers through his hair. He was thinking hard. 'Something like this, 'I' and then a blank for the prisoner's name, 'certify that Mark Durbin, of the Holborn Hotel in South Creek, is the true leader of the Creek Basin gang, and that Zeke Carver is the second in command.' That should do it, I think. Could you draft it out for us, Tom? I'd take it as a favour, if you would.'

The marshal soon went to work with paper and pen. He mouthed the message over again to make sure he had it right. For a moment or two more, Sam was on tenterhooks, in case anyone alerted the prisoners to the fact that Carver, and not Durbin, had done the recent shooting.

But his fears were now unfounded. Ferris brought the prisoners out again and himself witnessed their signatures at the bottom of the two statements. Spence was the first to hurry back into the cell. Sonora followed him.

Ferris remarked: 'Mark Durbin, eh? That'll be a shock for old Ellis Montford when he gets to hear it.'

'That's an understatement,' Sam replied. 'But right now, I want to get out of doors an' see if I have better luck in searchin' for the two missin' men.'

Ferris brought a stick of chewing tobacco out of his pocket. He hesitated before biting off the end. 'Sam, I hate to have to admit this, but I think there's a good chance both these two men are still in my town. I wish you luck.'

Sam thanked him and left. The fresh air out of doors was all that was still needed to clear his head after the recent fall. For an hour, he searched, without avail. Ellis Montford had left his hotel for a time, and no one knew where he was.

Similarly, Mark Durbin was nowhere around, and finally Zeke Carver was as elusive as ever. The deputized riders who had helped to round up Sonora and Spence made frequent short rides out from town, in an effort to find some sort of sign which suggested riders making a hurried getaway. They talked with travellers coming into town, but no one had seen anything of a suspicious nature.

One thing Sam did find out about the stolen money. It really had been removed from the safe, and there was no sort of evidence to show that it had been dropped out of the window.

Carver had gone, and, seemingly, the loot from the safe had gone with him. It was anybody's guess where Durbin was. Ferris would make sure that the rascally manager was not alerted by spreading gossip, but if he feared the worst — if he had sent Carver along to the peace office to do the shooting, where would he have gone himself?

He might have cleared out for good,

or he might be somewhere creating for himself an unbreakable alibi. Around tea time, Sam went back to the scene of the crime, but all was quiet again by then.

He found his way back to the office where he had kept watch, and very soon he was dozing on the inviting camp bed.

17

Around six o'clock, Sam began to come out of his deep sleep. His thoughts, contrarily, went back to Mirabelle Arnott. But this time the situation was a happier one. He was recollecting her last words to him before they parted. She had intimated that the Arnotts were not all likely to remain his enemies. She had been giving him hope, and he cherished that now, at a time when he was beginning to feel that his principal enemies had given him the slip.

One thing Sam knew for sure, he would never make any sort of a statement which would hurt the Arnott family concerning the memory and misdeeds of brother Pete. As far as he was concerned, Pete was dead and that was the end of it. The manner of Pete's death would gradually become insignificant.

Time would do a lot towards healing the breach between the Arnotts and himself. Time and the fair-mindedness and affection of Mirabelle.

But this was no time for thinking pretty thoughts. He still had to assume that the town harboured one or more dangerous criminals, and he had to resume the search which he had started earlier. There was only one place where he had not spread himself and that was the hotel itself.

When he had found Montford out, he had come away, being content to hear from the servants what had taken place. Now, he knew that he ought to go back to the building and search it from top to bottom. Intelligent criminals might still be using it, and he was the fellow to discover their hiding place before the general search grew lax and allowed them to escape.

★ ★ ★

Ellis Montford was very particular when it came to wine cellars. His basement rooms were always frequently white-washed and a dim lamp was kept burning in the main cellar throughout the daytime hours of work.

Sam Regan, who went below unattended, found this out for himself. He marvelled how like the basement of the East Halt hotel this one was, noted that the lamp wick had been recently trimmed and turned to peer into the semi-gloom of the lesser cellar.

As he did so, a very slight movement of some sort set his neck hairs rising. He might have disturbed a rat or lesser animal, but something had moved down there in the quiet depths. Moving with added caution and a hand on his gun, which was still holstered, he stepped further into the gloom and hurriedly surveyed the various racks.

A slight feeling of panic was making him draw his gun when a weighty body came from behind and pinned his arms to his sides. He filled his chest and braced himself, groping for he knew not what. By sheer good fortune, his questing left hand happened upon a wrist and closed on it. Closer than the wrist was the hand, and in the hand was a long-bladed knife, the point of which was only an inch or so away from his chest.

He hastily gripped the wrist which held the weapon with the other hand and at the same time swayed forward from his hips. His gun was still in the holster where it would have to remain until he thwarted the threat of the knife.

A violent twist of his body and a pulling down of the knife hand had the effect of swinging his attacker off balance. Zeke Carver went over his shoulder, brushed the side of the rack and dislodged two or three bottles. In landing, the outlaw did a somersault. He retained his grip upon the all-important knife and that brought Sam flying through the air after him.

They rolled on the floor, making very

little noise, each straining to get the upper hand in what was to be a fight to the death. Carver had failed to eliminate Sam once, but he did not intend to be found wanting this time.

Carver got into a good position and folded an arm round Sam's neck, seeking to choke the life out of him. All the time the knife hand swung backwards and forwards, held about a foot away from flesh.

Sam squirmed inside the throttling arm, turning his head towards the elbow. After thumping his adversary hard in the ribs with an elbow he contrived to slide his head out of trouble and turn his body at the same time.

At last they were facing each other, and Sam could see the determination in the close features of his attacker. Carver fought like a maniac, but his knife hand was being pushed very slowly nearer to his own chest. He made a big effort to pull his body from underneath and almost succeeded.

Sam hung on, and at the last moment the knife arm and grip of the defender caused the weapon to rip into its owner's chest. Carver reacted as though he had been stung. He released the hilt of the knife and threw Sam from him.

Moving like an automaton he clambered to his feet and entered the lighted cellar. He swayed there, at the foot of the stairs, and then started up them. Sam, badly shaken, scrambled to his feet and began to follow. Carver was about a third of the way up and crouching for some reason when the door at the top of the steps opened and a fair man in a derby hat and corduroys appeared there.

This newcomer hastily pulled his gun and fired two bullets into Carver's chest. The latter stepped back, lost his balance and fell dying into Sam's arms at the bottom.

The bulbous-eyed newcomer sighed with great satisfaction. He holstered his smoking gun and gestured towards Sam, who was still supporting the dead man.

'There, I figure I was jest in time to do you a big service, deputy. I was on the point of taking a look around for the outlaw, but I reckon you found him before I did.'

Sam nodded. 'Sure, you must be Mr Durbin, the manager of the Holborn Hotel in South Creek. I've been wantin' to make your acquaintance. Give me a minute an' I'll be with you.'

Sam lowered Carver to the ground, collected his fallen gun, and went on up the stairs. At the top Durbin extended his hand for a hand-shake, but he was greatly surprised when Sam advanced the gun towards him.

'Don't look so shocked, Mr Durbin. Altogether, three of your gang have testified that you are the real leader of the Creek Basin gang. We have you all now. Be good enough to stay right where you are for a few seconds. Don't go for that gun, please.'

Sam went back two or three stairs to where Carver had bent down. He fumbled around with his free hand and encountered a leather bag. At once he knew what it was. Carver had hidden the loot in a small recess beside the stairs. He had been bending to retrieve his ill-gotten gains when Durbin surprised him.

Gripping the bag in his free hand, Sam ran up the stairs again and casually took charge of the gun which had finished off Carver. He reflected once again that there was no honour between these two thieves.

In the foyer, he encountered the manager, Ellis Montford, and Marshal Tom Ferris. To the former, he surrendered the bag which held the loot and requested that the money should be checked over. To the latter, he said: 'Marshal, this is Mark Durbin, the renegade whose name appears on those documents in your office. Maybe you'd like to take him along to lock him up. He jest shot Carver down below.'

Ferris took over without comment. Durbin, who was still speechless, had an expression on his face which showed that he accepted defeat.

For several minutes, Sam stood alone on the steps of the foyer. His fingers were busy with his tobacco sack, but his mind was busy with the contents of a fairly long triumphal telegraph message intended for Sheriff Moses Wallis.

THE END

We do hope that you have enjoyed reading this large print book.

Did you know that all of our titles are available for purchase?

We publish a wide range of high quality large print books including:
Romances, Mysteries, Classics
General Fiction
Non Fiction and Westerns

Special interest titles available in large print are:
The Little Oxford Dictionary
Music Book, Song Book
Hymn Book, Service Book

Also available from us courtesy of Oxford University Press:
Young Readers' Dictionary
(large print edition)
Young Readers' Thesaurus
(large print edition)

For further information or a free brochure, please contact us at:
Ulverscroft Large Print Books Ltd.,
The Green, Bradgate Road, Anstey,
Leicester, LE7 7FU, England.
Tel: (00 44) **0116 236 4325**
Fax: (00 44) **0116 234 0205**

The stage robbery had been accomplished by an old woman. Twine Fourch had never heard of a female being a highway robber before. He followed the trail all the way to a dilapidated log cabin up Stone Mountain. What happened after that no one could believe even after townsmen from Jefferson found the old log house and the skeletal dying old woman. But before the mystery could be solved there would be two unnecessary killings, a bizarre suicide and a lynching.

GUNS OF THE GAMBLER

M. Duggan

Destitute gambler Ben Crow arrives in Mallory keen to claim his inheritance, only to discover that rancher Edward Bacon has other ideas. Set up by Miss Dorothy, who had fooled him completely, Ben finds himself dangling on the end of a rope. Saved from death, Ben sets off in pursuit of Miss Dorothy, determined upon retribution. However, his quest for vengeance turns into a rescue mission when she is kidnapped by a crazy man-burning bandit.

SIDEWINDER

John Dyson

All Flynn wants is to be Marshal of Tucson, but he is framed by the territory's richest rancher, Frank Buchanan, and thrown into Yuma prison. Five years later Flynn comes out, intent on clearing his name and burning for vengeance. Fists thud, knives flash and bullets fly as he rides both sides of the law and participates in kidnapping and double-dealing. He is once again arrested for a murder of which he is innocent. Can he escape the noose a second time?

THE BLOODING OF JETHRO

Frank Fields

When Jethro Smith's family is murdered by outlaws, vengeance is the one thing on his mind. He meets the brother of one of the murderers, who attempts to exploit Jethro's grudge in the pursuit of his own vendetta. The local preacher, formerly a sheriff, teaches Jethro how to use a gun. With his new-found skills, Jethro and his somewhat unwelcome friend pit themselves against seemingly impossible odds. Whatever the outcome lead would surely fly.

SEVEN HELLS AND A SIXGUN

Jack Greer

Jim Cayman had been warned about Daphne Rankin, his boss's wife, and her little ways. When Daphne made a play for Jim and he resisted, the result was painful and about what he had feared. But suddenly matters went beyond the expected and he found himself left to die an awful death. Only then did he realise that there was far more than a woman scorned. He vowed that if he could escape from the hell-hole he would surely solve the mystery — and settle some scores.

CRISIS IN CASTELLO COUNTY

D. A. Horncastle

The first thing Texas Ranger Sergeant Brad Saunders finds when he responds to an urgent call for help from the local sheriff is the corpse of the public prosecutor floating in the Nueces River. Soon Brad finds himself caught in the midst of a power struggle between a gang of tough western outlaws and a bunch of Italian gangsters, whose thirst for bloody revenge knows no bounds. Brad was going to have all his work cut out to end the bloody warfare — and stay alive!